The Donor

By

Stevie Turner

The Donor

Thanks to Caleb's Book Formatting Services for tidying my manuscript.

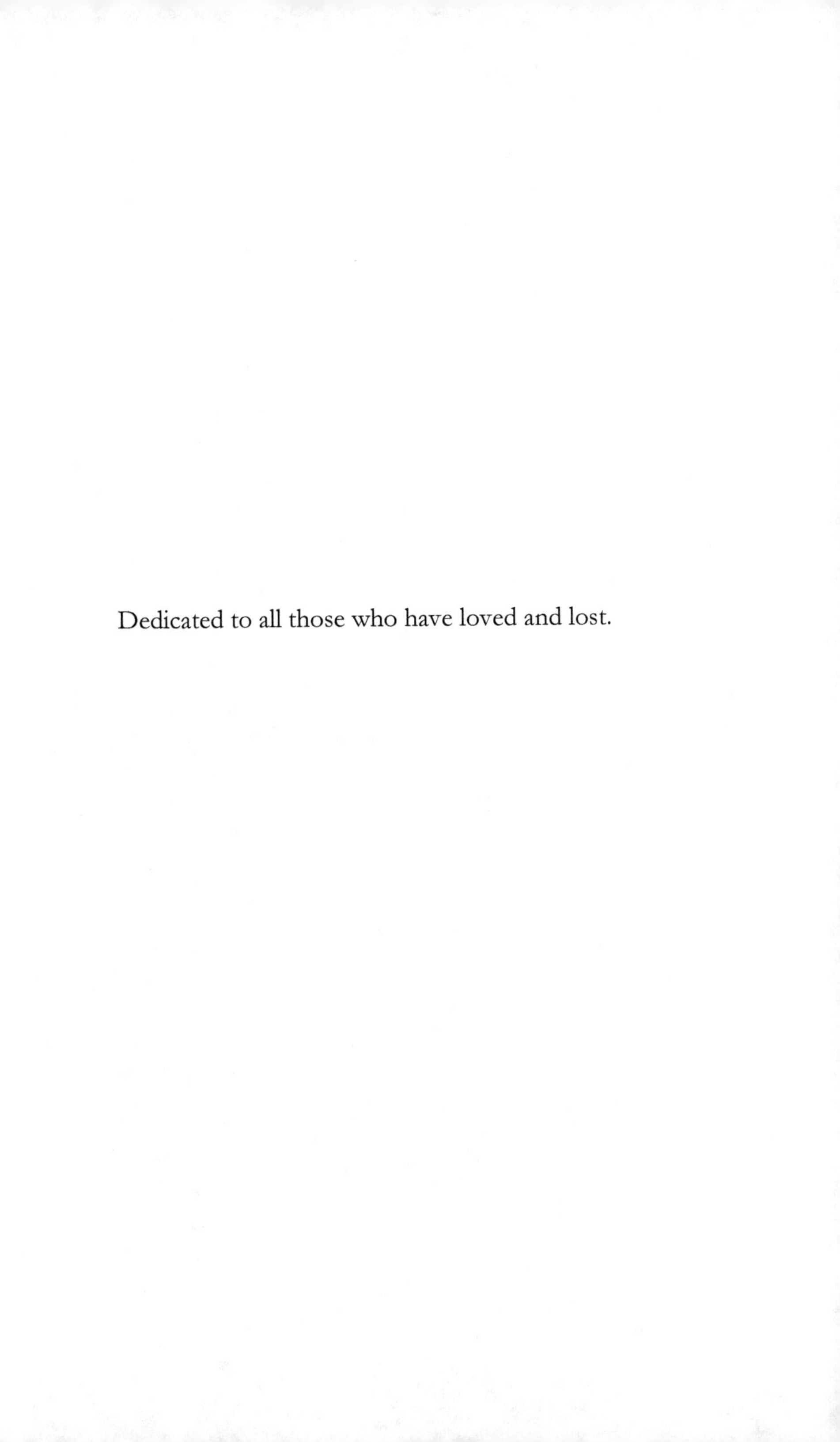

Dedicated to all those who have loved and lost.

SYNOPSIS

When you know you have met the love of your life, the last thing you expect is for your sister to lure him away. Clare Ronson is faced with this scenario when her sister Isabel marries singer and guitarist Ross Tyler. To compound Clare's jealousy and bitterness, Ross hits the big time and becomes a wealthy tax exile, relocating to France with his family. Clare cannot bring herself to speak to Isabel or Ross for the next 30 years. However, when tragedy occurs in 2002 causing Ross to arrive back in England at Clare's doorstep, Clare must try to put the past behind her for her sister's sake.

Table of Contents

CHAPTER 1 - 1970

CLARE

LIFE AS I know it is definitely starting to be a bit of a drag, due to the fact that I've been awake now for 3 days and nights on Desolation Hill. I am finished, *kaput*. Thank God it's the last day, that's all I can say.

I yawn for the umpteenth time and watch in a kind of stupor as the fences are torn down. Ruth jumps up excitedly and decides that she wants to try and get nearer the stage. I watch her treading unconcerned over zombie-like bodies lying comatose and frying in the heat of the late August afternoon, and try to summon up enough strength to follow her. But by then, hungrier and more tired than I have ever been, I am faced with the certainty that all I really want to do is to go home. Bands have started to merge one into the other, but I know I'll have to face a ribbing from Ruth if I set off without first having tried to get nearer the stage if only to feast *one* weary eye on the hunk of masculinity that is Paul Rogers while there is still some good daylight left.

I force my body to move, performing a quick recce around what has transformed in three days from arable farmland into a nuclear fallout zone contained in some kind of human landfill site. I cannot see Ruth, but I stumble on regardless. Somewhere out there my friend has become lost in a sea of 500,000 faces; just another flower-bedecked hippie indistinguishable from the masses.

Far away on the horizon I can see a speck holding a microphone stand up above his head; Paul Rogers is holding the crowd in the palm of his hand, and I am missing it. Behind him on the low stage, long hair flying in the sultry air, Paul Kossoff, six string shredder extraordinaire, is ripping into the solo for 'All Right Now.'

I cannot make my legs walk another step. I yawn. Infuriatingly I still seem to be on Desolation Hill as far as I can make out. Sighing with fatigue, I slump down on the grass where I stand, close my eyes, and listen to the hubbub around me. My long hair feels like a heavy blanket on my back; I desperately want something to eat, I need a bath, and I ache for my mum to be fussing around me like she does when I am sick.

"Hey babe, have some of this."

I am startled by a voice very close to my ear. I open my eyes again and look to my left to see what only can be described as a bronzed, blond Adonis, with long fair curls stretching down over his shoulders. He is stripped to the waist apart from a small rucksack on his back, and wears frayed pale-blue Levi shorts and a pair of well-worn 'Jesus creeper' sandals. He squats down beside me and holds out a lighted spliff.

"It'll take away the pain."

I consider myself to be *in extremis*, soon to be engulfed in the Grim Reaper's arms. There is no way out except death. I take a huge drag and retch as the sweet fumes of cannabis grab the back of my throat.

"Thanks." I cough. "I think."

"Woh!" Adonis laughs into the sun. "Easy! You're not used to it, I can tell."

"Is it that obvious?" I want my head to stop spinning. "I've come to the end of my rope. A spliff won't do any harm now." I take another drag.

"I think I'll take it back actually." Adonis prises the joint from my fingers. "Are you hungry?"

"Starving." I nod, with eyes trying to close. "All I've got left is my hovercraft ticket back to Southsea."

"And you can't eat that." Adonis attacks the spliff with expertise, puffing out a cloud of aromatic smoke. "I'll see what I've got left in my rucksack."

Keeping the spliff between the index and middle finger of his left hand, with one poetic swoop of his right shoulder he dislodges the rucksack's straps, opens it up and looks inside, bringing out a slightly dented but still crisp-looking Golden Delicious apple and handing it to me.

"My mum's always on at me to eat more roughage." Laughing, I feast my eyes on the apple, which in my famished state seems to have taken on the proportions of a gargantuan banquet.

"If you're sure." I cannot help but take it. "I've eaten nothing since yesterday. Somebody stole what was left of my food. It's too far to walk to try and buy some, and anyway, I've no money left."

"It's every man for himself, here." Adonis nods. "What's your name?"

"Clare." I bite into pure nectar. "Clare Ronson. How about you?"

"Hi Clare, I'm Ross Tyler." Adonis holds out his hand. "I hitchhiked from Ryde on Friday with a mate from college, who was last seen yesterday trying to find somewhere private to take a crap."

Juice from the apple runs down my chin and I wipe it away with my left hand, shake Ross's hand with the other, and smile up at him.

"You're a lifesaver, Ross. I came here with a friend as well, but maybe she met up with your mate. I haven't seen her for a few hours now."

"Looks like it's us two against the world then." Ross slings the rucksack back over his shoulder. "I'm on my way up the hill; going to hitchhike back to Ryde and get a chance on the hovercraft before this lot set off. Coming?"

I've had enough. My knight in Jesus creepers has materialised and is standing right in front of me. Not one for wanting to look a gift horse in the mouth, and fortified by the sweet fruit, I nod and get to my feet.

"Yes; I want to go home."

Paul Rogers is giving it all he's got. Taking one last look at the stage and wondering if I would ever see the like of it again, I grab my saviour's outstretched hand and we begin to thread our way between the bodies and mounds of detritus, back up Desolation Hill and over Afton Down, eventually descending onto the Military Road. Crowds of young people have the same idea, and we all saunter along amiably in the late afternoon heat, in no rush to get off the Island, and unaware that we are part of history in the making. In front of us are two girls holding hands; one is naked except for a pair of pink knickers, and the other is bare from the waist down.

"Looks like those two have fared worse than you." Ross smirks.

I am stoned on cannabis fumes, lack of sleep, hunger, and a definite animal attraction for my new-found friend. It matters to me not one jot that female flesh usually kept under wraps is now exposed to the stares of all and sundry. Presently the girls slope off and join many other festival-goers, washing off the dirt from Desolation Hill in the choppy waters of Freshwater Bay. I smile at Ross as we trudge along Military Road, copying him and raising my thumb some time later as crowds begin to thin out and the odd car can be seen driving past us on the way to maybe Brook Green or further on into Niton or Newport.

"Who in their right mind is going to give *us* a lift?" I panic while wondering just how much further I can walk. "Look at the state of us. How many miles is it to Ryde from here? Can't we wait for a bus?"

"About twenty." Comes the cheerful reply. "I'm skint, the same as you. It's hitching or Shanks's pony."

My affable, blond Adonis is prepared to traipse into the night to reach his destination. It's all I can do to keep up with his long, loping strides. The buzz from the apple wears off around Compton Bay, and I want to cry.

"Cheer up, babe."

Ross winks and puts his arm around me. The effect is galvanising and instantly spurs me on. I gaze up into his pale blue eyes, and his nearness causes a pleasant throbbing sensation in my groin. I have never seen such beauty in a man before. I am certain I haven't seen him at Uni.

"Which University are you at?" I find myself looking down in the direction of his groin as we walk.

"Not Uni; Portsmouth Art College." Ross holds his fist up and jerks his thumb at passing cars. "How about you?"

"The Uni; not far from there though. Reading English; I

want to be a teacher. Do you think you'll be a famous painter then?"

"Don't know." Ross shrugs and fondles the hair at the back of my neck. "But I'm having a ball finding out."

It's not until we walk past Compton Bay and head towards Brook Green that a van stops next to us. Ross is still pointing his thumb in the vague direction of Newport, but I have long ago given up, and am just concentrating on putting one foot in front of the other. I hear Ross speak to the driver who is on his way to Bembridge, and to my great delight he beckons us into the cab and agrees to drop us off along the seafront at Ryde. The van has three seats at the front. I let Ross go in first, who chats amiably to the driver most of the way I think. Me, I put my head on Ross's shoulder and am asleep before the van has even pulled away.

CHAPTER 2

ROSS

AS STONED AS I am that day in the chaos of Desolation Hill I can see her standing out from the rest, with that ethereal, new-born fawn fragility that always seems to appeal to a man's protective instinct. I watch her as wounded, she collapses to the ground, oblivious to her surroundings. I want to gather her up in my arms there and then and never let her go.

I have to make sure I'm not treading on anybody's toes; you know what I mean, don't you? Has another bloke already laid claim? I look about but she seems to be on her own. I'm on my way back to Ryde; the festival hasn't really lived up to my expectations, but when I find Clare I know the whole experience of living in shit for three days has been well worth it.

She isn't used to weed, that's obvious. She seems unsullied; shiny as a new pin. I wonder if she's experienced in the ways of the world so to speak, but for now that will have to wait. I assume the latter, as she looks only about 18 or 19 and is still rather shy. I'll have to tread carefully in that department; when I'd been that age I'd already put it about quite a bit, but I don't think it's the same for girls, although thankfully more of them are on the pill in these enlightened days.

I want to see her again. She sleeps most of the way to Ryde with her head on my shoulder. The driver is a fucking bore; all he talks about is top dressing his fields with lime before the next wheat crops go in. I want him to shut up so that I can concentrate on holding Clare, but have to pretend to listen. I don't really give a shit about soil testing, pH levels and screened lime, but I learn all about it anyway and hey, who knows, it might even come in handy one day.

She wakes up as we drive down Argyll Street. She seems a bit embarrassed to have been asleep so long, and sits up apologetically. I give her shoulder a quick squeeze before letting her go.

"We're nearly at Ryde seafront."

"Oh God; sorry to have conked out like that."

She gives me a beautiful smile. Even the old farmer seems taken with her, and keeps glancing her way when he really needs to be looking at the road. Me, I am gutted that our journey is coming to an end. I don't mind if the farmer drives us around and around the Island *ad infinitum* until we disappear up the van's exhaust pipe just for the continued chance of holding her close for another few hours.

There is already a huge crowd of festival-goers at the hovercraft terminal when we climb out of the van, so I know there's going to be a long wait. Clare is yawning and dazed, and slumps down on a nearby seat. I take her ticket, go into the terminal, queue up and book our seats on the 20:45

hovercraft. I am conscious of the fact that the ride back to Southsea only takes 10 minutes, and I know that if I do not look sharp she will soon be slipping through my fingers.

Some bastard is chatting her up when I get back to the seat. I take both of her hands in mine, pull her up, and guide her over to the sea wall where we can sit in relative privacy.

"We've got about an hour to wait. I'd buy you a cup of tea, but I don't have any money." I laugh.

"That's okay." She looks around. "I'm going to find a phone box and make a reverse charge call; I'll ask my mum to get Dad to pick me up at Southsea. He doesn't know where I've been, but I'll talk him round."

"I'll come with you; there's toilets along there." I point towards the other side of the terminal. "There might even be a drinking fountain inside as well."

The phone box is up near St. Thomas' Street. She disappears inside and speaks animatedly to person or persons unknown. I stand alone on the pavement suddenly jealous of the family who are waiting for her on the other side, eager to take her back to the fold and away from me. Presently she comes out grinning and is seemingly wide awake.

"Mum said my dad will set off for the Southsea terminal in about half an hour. Do you need to phone anyone?"

"Nah; I can walk home from there." I shake my head. "I'm okay."

"It's no trouble; I'll get Dad to give you a lift."

I don't fancy the idea of meeting her father and having him look down on me when he sees the state of the outside of our house. In my experience, Dads on the whole do not take kindly to their daughters running around with the likes of me.

The long hair puts them off for a start, and when they find out that not only do I sing and play guitar in a rock band, but I also attend Art College, it seems to drive the wedge in a bit further. I suppose they are on the lookout for a future bank manager son-in-law for their little princesses; unfortunately there I come up a bit short. The idea of spending the rest of my days in some back office poring over dusty ledgers appals me to the point where I know I'd rather be dead than have to live that way.

It will be easy to sidle out of the lift. However, the next item on my agenda might prove to be rather trickier. As we walk back towards the toilets on the seafront I screw up my courage and take her hand.

"How do you feel about us meeting up again after tonight? We don't live that far apart. I sing in a band; you could come and watch if you like. We've got a gig next Friday at the Wig and Pen."

There is a few seconds of silence while she digests the information, and then I feel her squeeze my hand:

"If I wake up in time; I think I'm going to sleep for a week."

Yes! She wants to see me again! I try not to show too much enthusiasm, but actually I am over the moon.

"Great; my older brother Darryl is the drummer; then there's Chaz the bassist, and Andy plays lead. I'll get Darryl to drive his van over and pick you up a couple of hours before. I've got a biro in my rucksack; hang on." I swing the rucksack around to the front and take out a pen. "Write your address on my arm."

"It's all hairy." She giggles.

I turn my arm over and she begins to write on the white underside of my forearm. The gentle fluttering strokes of the pen feel somehow strangely erotic, and it's all I can do to stop myself ravishing her there and then on the pavement.

"It'll be a great evening." Regardless of my hard-on I pull her to me when she has finished writing. "I'm glad I've met you."

"Me too." She smiles shyly at me.

I kiss her opposite the Tourist Information Centre, and then once again by the sea wall before I disappear into the toilets to relieve both my bladder and also by now my somewhat embarrassing erection.

We don't speak much on the hovercraft. The overall atmosphere is subdued, with glassy-eyed revellers swiftly coming to the conclusion that the festival is over and that the real world will be beckoning them in a few hours' time. Clare rests her head on my shoulder and holds my hand as we bounce over the waves, waving to her father as we exit the hovercraft a few minutes' later, who is already waiting for her up on the road. *Bastard.* It's time to make myself scarce.

CHAPTER 3

CLARE

THE GOOD THING about being off from University is the ability to sleep in past noon. It's about half past one when I wake up on the Monday afternoon, the last day of August. Mum and Dad went off to work hours earlier at the hospital, and Izzy is probably still down in London staying with friends. I have the house to myself.

I stretch luxuriously and find a cool spot for my toes at the end of the bed. Mum pointed me in the direction of the shower as soon as I returned home, and then stuffed me full of roast dinner, so I am not especially hungry when I wake up. I think my stomach must have shrunk at the festival.

I take my time in running a hot bubble bath and having a soak, and think about Ross as I lay there soaping myself. I still tingle from his kisses, and am left in no doubt that he finds me attractive. I wonder about how to broach the subject with Mum that I want to start taking the pill. I know that Izzy has been on it for a few years and is having a wild time of it down in London unbeknownst to Dad, who thinks she's the absolute epitome of a conscientious medical student. Mum knows what goes on though because she and Izzy are close, but Izzy is three years older than me. At 22 she has her pick of drooling men, but Ross will be my first ever boyfriend.

Eventually I decide I'll say nothing to Mum, and will go along to book an appointment with the GP in secret, and start the process of losing my infuriatingly cumbersome virginity. As I lay there in the bath I feel a thrill of excitement at the thought of making love with Ross. Izzy always has that world-weary air about her when telling me that sex is no big deal, but I remain convinced of the fact that when I give myself to Ross it will be by far the most momentous occasion that has ever happened in my life.

I finish washing and step out of the bath, admire my suntan in the mirror and sing softly whilst wrapping myself in a towel. A sound outside on the landing startles me, and I open the bathroom door to peek out. Izzy stands facing me in her baby doll nightdress, brilliant and belligerent, with long, shiny dark hair and midnight blue eyes making her drop-dead gorgeous as usual, even though she has obviously just got out of bed.

"What are you so happy about?"

I had no idea that my sister has returned home, but I can't help but grin at her question.

"I think I've got a boyfriend." I pirouette in the towel for extra effect.

"Whoop-de-do; Miss Virgin Mary finally finds out what it's all about." Izzy brushes past me, lifts up her nightie and sits down on the toilet. "Have you got any tampons? Thank

God I think my period's starting; for a moment there it was touch and go."

I try not to show the shock I feel at my sister's implication of a possible pregnancy. She is a third year medical student; our father would have been beside himself with fury.

"They're in the top drawer of my dressing table. Help yourself."

I leave her sitting on the toilet and go into my bedroom to find some clean clothes. The sullied festival shorts and t-shirt are still on the floor where I had thrown them the night before. I pick them up with the secret knowledge that Ross has actually touched my t-shirt, and I hold it to my chest before placing it in the laundry basket. No boy has ever affected me in the way that Ross has, and I don't know how I'm going to make it to Friday evening without exploding with longing and frustration.

Izzy barges in without knocking, just as I drop the towel and look for a clean pair of knickers.

"So come on then, out with it." She opens my dressing table drawer and takes a Tampax out of the box. "Who is he? Where did you meet him?"

"He saved me from dying at the Isle of Wight festival." I sigh. "I'd run out of food and money, and he got me back home."

"Silly cow." Izzy shakes her head. "What happened to Ruth?"

"We got split up, but I'm glad we did now." I chuckle. "Ross is an art student at Portsmouth College, *and* he sings in a band and plays rhythm guitar." I add the last bit for extra effect.

"Mum and Dad are just going to *lurrrve* him...." Izzy trails off and looks at me. "My God! You're in love!"

"Yes I am." I couldn't help smiling. "I know I've only just met him, but he's the most beautiful thing I've ever seen. If you're about on Friday you'll see him; he's coming round with his brother to pick me up in their van. They've got a gig at the Wig and Pen."

"You didn't do it in a tent, did you? Are you on the pill?"

There she goes again doing her 'I'm-a-woman-of-the-world-and-you-know-nothing' big sister act. I always find her patronising attitude to be quite infuriating, but this time through good humour can brush it off without it erupting into an argument.

I find some clean underwear and look in the wardrobe for a dress.

"Mind your own biz, but no and no actually."

"Get down the doctors then, in case Percy pops out of his pocket."

She has a way with words, and I can't help laughing at the mental image this conjures up. Izzy grins, and suddenly we both clutch each other and giggle like two schoolgirls.

"Bash the bloody thing if it comes out!" Izzy roars. "Or knee him in the balls!"

"Good advice, but no...." I laugh. "We haven't got to that stage yet anyway."

"Just be careful." Izzy gives me a hug and made for the door. "You know what I mean."

"Did you think *you* were pregnant, Iz? I look at her retreating back as I zip up my favourite purple midi-dress, which always makes me feel very bohemian when I wear it. Today I want to be reminded of the festival, and Ross:

"Yeah; but the worst of it is that I didn't even know who the father was." Izzy exhales with force and turns around briefly. "I got drunk after the exams finished and woke up next to Adrian Lister, who normally I wouldn't touch with somebody else's barge pole, let alone my own."

"What about Jeff?" I wonder if her boyfriend had found out.

"Jeff who? Adrian probably boasted about it all around the campus, and Jeff found out and pissed off."

"Oh, Izzy, I'm sorry!" My mouth forms a little 'o' of dismay. "I know you liked him."

"Forget it." I shrug the remark away. "There's plenty more fish in the sea."

It seems strange at the role reversal in that I am now the one with the boyfriend. My sister has had a succession of male friends since the age of about 15, although it has always been Jeff who has lasted the longest of all of them. I wonder what she will think of Ross if she is still around on Friday night.

CHAPTER 4

IZZY

I HOPE I'VE kept the real misery of the break-up with Jeff from Clare; all those dreadful weeks of recriminations, and my futile tears and apologies. Eventually I decide to make the most of the summer break and race home with my tail between my legs, but always in the back of my mind is the stark fact that I have to face Jeff again when the new term begins. I'm not really looking forward to another three years of studying, and it's nice to just to be home and have nothing to do. Mum and Dad are pleased to see me of course, but they don't know the real reason I've come back. Clare is away for the weekend, so I manage to find some time alone with Mum and pour my heart out. Mum says things would blow over, but I'm not so sure.

It's quite nice being home again, but I can only stand it for a short while because Mum loves fussing over Clare and me as though we were still five years old. Clare's trying to grow up I can see, but Mum and Dad still baby her somewhat. It's not good for her, so perhaps this new boyfriend coming on the scene will convince them that she's nineteen now, not nine. I suppose that's the problem when the youngest child is the only one left at home; Mum doesn't want to admit that we've grown up and have lives of our own away from them.

I spilled the beans to Mum about Clare's boyfriend. I know I shouldn't have done it, but Clare hasn't let on to our parents that he will be turning up on their doorstep on Friday night. Mum promises she won't say anything until Clare mentions it, but then goes on to ask her if she met anybody at the festival. Clare glares at me as soon as Mum goes to work with *that* look, and I *know* what's coming.

"Why did you tell her about Ross?"

Clare looks about as happy as somebody undergoing a PR investigation. I shrug and make light of it.

"I didn't." Lying comes easily after the fiasco with Adrian. "Perhaps she was just interested in what you'd been up to."

"They won't like him. I wasn't going to say anything and just let him turn up."

Clare looks worried. My curiosity is aroused even further, and so I try to probe a little bit deeper.

"What about him is going to put them off?" I ask as casually as I can.

"The long hair for a start, but I've never seen such hair on a man before." Clare's eyes look misty. "It's curly and blond and comes down over his shoulders."

"She sounds like she should be plucking a harp and floating on a cloud."

The sarcasm isn't lost on my sister. She's very quick on the uptake; it's a family trait.

"*He's* far from cherubic. *He* smokes weed, and the Art College thing isn't Dad's cup of tea, let's face it."

"Good luck with that then." I suddenly want to meet this weed-smoking cherub. "You're going to need it."

We are eating supper when the doorbell rings. Clare has hardly touched her food, and looks constantly towards the clock above the Aga as she pushes carrots and peas around her plate. Dad appears totally unconcerned at her behaviour; I expect Mum hasn't mentioned Ross to him at all.

She jumps up like a startled rabbit to open the door and virtually runs, long brown ponytail swishing from side to side as she picks up speed down the hallway. I turn my head to try and catch a glimpse of Blondie, and from what I can see he is definitely a force to be reckoned with; tall and tanned, with angular features and clean looking curly, almost white-blond hair reaching indeed a little past his shoulders. However, the long hair, the scruffy jeans, and the t-shirt and bomber jacket marks him out straight away as *the enemy* in my parents' eyes, and I know that within a short time the shit is going to hit the fan.

He follows her up to where we sit in the kitchen. He looks amazing, and I drop some peas off my fork as I take a long second look. His eyes meet mine, and in that brief second I see longing, and the kind of hunger that Clare will never be able to satisfy. I tear my eyes away and look towards Dad, who has put down his knife and fork and is looking up at Ross with an obvious deep disdain.

"Hi." Blondie keeps his face expressionless and waits for a reaction.

"Who's this?" Dad looks accusingly at Clare, as though

she is ready to elope to Gretna Green.

"This is my friend, Ross. We met at the festival." Clare is smiling at Dad so nervously that it appears as a grimace. "We've got to go now because he's got a gig with his band tonight."

"Go where?" Dad stands up to give Ross the once over.

"To the Wig and Pen in Portsmouth. Ross's brother has a van outside."

"Hello Mr Ronson." Ross pipes up. "I'll take good care of her, don't worry."

"It's *Doctor* Ronson actually." Dad's face is grim as he begins to assert his authority. "*And* I'll be picking her up at ten thirty."

"Cool." Ross nods, totally unfazed.

"See you all later." Clare grabs her bag and the two of them leave.

It's not until pudding that Dad lets out a sigh.

"I don't like the look of him." He shakes his head. "Bloody long-haired layabout."

"Give him a chance, Donald." Mum uses her best appeasing tone. "Clare seems quite taken with him."

"Well, he's not getting his feet under *my* table. Look at the state of him!" Dad barks. "And why didn't somebody tell me she was going to that bloody festival! I thought she was staying with Ruth!"

"Well, *I* didn't know." I shrug. "I only came home on Saturday."

"Marian – did you know where she was?" Dad glares at Mum.

"No idea." Mum manages to lie as easily as I can. "Not until she phoned."

"We'll have to put her on a shorter leash." Dad pours custard over his treacle tart. "We can't have her running around with the likes of him."

"She's nineteen." Mum smiles at him. "We have to let her make her own mistakes."

"Next thing you know he'll have got her in the family way. She'll throw away her life and end up in some filthy squat, that's for certain! Where does he work?"

Dad is really getting into his stride now. I can see that poor old Ross has been hung, drawn and quartered before he's even had a chance to prove his worth. I remember those baby blue eyes, pregnant indeed with hidden promises and desires.

"He's an art student at the college as well as being in the band." I watch Dad's face for the expected reaction.

"Jesus H Christ!" Dad throws his spoon down onto the table. "That settles it! I'll give her a piece of my mind when I pick her up!"

I look at Mum, but she isn't giving anything away. It is impossible to talk rationally to Dad when he is in one of his moods. I finish my pudding quickly, and escape upstairs as soon as ever I can.

CHAPTER 5

MARIAN

I'VE NEVER SEEN Clare so enamoured of someone before. She walks around in a dream with a smile on her face most of the time. It's hard to be cross with her; she reminds me of myself when I met Donald 25 years ago, and even though her father is laying down the law I can see it's going in one ear and out the other.

I trust my youngest daughter implicitly. Isabel was always the wild one, but Clare has very high morals and scruples, unusual in this day and age. She wants to 'save herself' for marriage I think, which is quite admirable to say the least. Even if Ross *is* trying to get her to change her mind, I'm sure Clare will stay steadfastly against sex before marriage to stay true to herself.

I quite liked the boy when I saw him that one time. He must have picked up on Donald's negative vibes though I'm sure, because he no longer comes to the house. Clare says she is visiting Ruth, but Isabel has seen her in the van with

Ross and his brother several times. I think Isabel wants to sneak off to one of the band's gigs, but I told her not to tell her father if she does decide to go.

I'm trying to get through to Donald, but he's like a bear with a sore head; unwilling to let Clare grow up and learn through her own mistakes. I know no good can come of this liaison but Ross is her first love, but I remember myself how I felt all those years ago; emotions can be overpowering for a young girl. She often speaks of him to me, and is so in love I can't bear to disillusion her.

I want to tell her about Eric, but somehow it doesn't seem right to talk about a man I love who isn't her father. I have never stopped loving Eric, but the relationship wasn't to be. I had my own scruples in those days, and was terrified of becoming pregnant. The girls have it easy now; there's the contraceptive pill which wasn't available 30 years ago, but I'm not sure it's doing much for their morals. To be able to sleep around with multiple partners is not good for a girl's reputation; it's bringing a different kind of shame upon the family now isn't it? Eric wanted a full relationship before marriage, but it went against the values I'd been brought up with. Donald was one of the few men I'd met who was prepared to wait, surprising indeed considering his rampant sexual appetite, but then again when I've thought about that over the years I have come to the conclusion that although the brakes were on for *me,* the accelerator was probably flat to the floor with all the others.

However, should I tell her that actually all the waiting is not worth it? She's on cloud 9 imagining her wedding night I'm sure, but from personal experience and listening in the delivery suite all these years to stories I've heard from my patients, most of them only report the same as I; pain and disappointment. The sex act with a new partner takes months to perfect, and as I've matured I am now of a different opinion. If a girl has an engagement ring on her finger, then she should make use of the pill and start finding out what pleasures her and her partner can enjoy. Isabel I know took this viewpoint seriously even without the engagement ring, and so far, thankfully, she has managed to avoid a pregnancy. Clare, bless her, has always been quite shocked that her sister sleeps around so much. Donald has no idea that Isabel does not spend her entire free time studying Grey's Anatomy, and I for one am not going to enlighten him. However, his eldest daughter always learns quickly and attains mostly high marks and soaks up information like a sponge, although I worry about her not seemingly having the patience and motivation needed to become a successful doctor. I wonder if she is studying medicine just to please her father. I imagine she has plenty of free time to get up to all sorts of mischief whilst her peers are poring over their textbooks.

Isabel tells me that she is going along with Clare to watch Ross's band. I'm not sure why, but warning bells have started to ring in my head. Isabel is still getting over the break-up with Jeff, and I think is rather vulnerable at the moment. She's never been that interested before in going around with her younger sister, and it worries me somewhat. Clare is over-the-moon in love with the boy, and as far as I can tell he seems to feel the same way about her. They need to spend time on their own and find out about each other, without anybody else on the scene. Isabel is sexually mature, and knows how to use the assets that God gave her to her best advantage. To my knowledge Jeff hasn't phoned, so I think I'll need to have a quiet word with Isabel just to make sure she is going along for the company and nothing else. The last thing I want is a summer of discontent.

The girls seem closer than they used to be. I think perhaps this is because Isabel is making stronger efforts to get along with Clare. It's nice to see them giggling together, and Isabel advising her younger sister about make-up and the right sort of clothes to wear. The three years between them used to be a kind of chasm when they were younger, but now they actually seem fond of one another. I remember acting as referee for years; God, the whining, backbiting and tale-telling made me want to fling open the front door and make a run for it sometimes, but of course I never did. As soon as he came home, a raised forefinger and one look from Donald would cause Clare to dissolve, but more often than not he would be at the hospital and so it was down to me to sort out the arguments. Isabel always used to stare her father out and make him even madder, but she soon found out that his bark was worse than his bite. He never laid a hand on them in anger, and sometimes I tired of it always being myself who had to lay down the law.

It's nice now that my relationship with Isabel and Clare has changed from a mother trying to keep the peace between them to more like one of a friend and advisor. Donald still tries to dominate them and bark out instructions as to who they can or cannot go about with, but they're well past that age where Dad flapping his arms about and dictating does any good. I know that neither of them are listening to him now, and are just going their own way, which is as it should be. If Donald knew half of the things that his daughters are getting up to, I wouldn't put it past him to try and chain them to a radiator until they behave. Well, perhaps that's a trifle dramatic, but I *know* he would be so rude to Ross if he ever had the temerity to show his face here again.

Clare has it down to a fine art. At a pre-arranged time the van will pull up at the end of the street out of Donald's line of vision, and off she will go after hugging me and giving her father a kiss goodbye and telling him she is going to visit Ruth. This Saturday night both girls will be leaving at the same time, as Isabel has suddenly developed a fascination with rock music. I will definitely need to speak to her alone very soon and make sure that she knows just how deeply in love Clare and Ross seem to be.

CHAPTER 6

ISABEL

I'M NOT QUITE sure if Clare's said anything to Mum regarding not being happy about me tagging along when the band play on Saturday night. Clare hasn't mentioned any worries to me, and I'm sure she would do if she wanted to be on her own with Ross, and so Mum suddenly wittering on about leaving them alone came as rather a surprise.

Jeff hasn't phoned and I'm feeling a bit unloved and lonely. I've even been reduced to revising *symphysis pubis dystocia* for the next exams at Christmas; it's bloody boring! I *need* a night out. I want to drown my sorrows in a pint or three of beer and listen to some music that isn't Mum's Mantovani orchestra or Perry *Coma*; good God they sound like they need a squib up their collective rectums.

I've bought one of those floaty tops for Saturday, and I think I can still get into my skin-tight jeans after a couple of weeks of Mum's cooking. The trick is to lay down and put them on; I don't know how it works, but probably the abdomen is flatter in the prone position and it's easier to pull them up. I'll pile on the mascara and give myself some Dusty Springfield eyes as well. Jeff said it was my eyes that he first noticed (and then the tits came afterwards).

Jeff. Am I over him? The answer is *no*, but with each day that passes I'm feeling more optimistic about my future. I'm only 22, and am veering towards Mum's advice that there's lots more fish in the sea. Whether I'll find anybody who's on my wavelength on Saturday remains to be seen, but I intend to have a good time finding out.

Clare takes ages to get ready before she meets up with Blondie; it reminds me of when Jeff and I first started going out. Now that Saturday night's here I'm feeling ever so slightly envious of my younger sister; so in love and with that *all's right with the world* look about her.

I pour myself into my jeans and find a pair of red stilettos. The salmon pink low-necked top looks good I must admit, and as I brush my hair I look at my reflection in the mirror and feel pleased with the result of my efforts. My dark hair shines, my eyes look like Dusty's, and I've still got a bit of a tan. I toss my hair back and apply some lipstick; I want to turn some heads tonight.

Dad's downstairs when Clare whispers to me that the van is outside. I throw a jacket over my shoulders to conceal a multitude of sins. Clare's buttoned up like Miss Vestal Virgin 1970, and she even gives Dad a kiss on the cheek.

"Where are you two off to then?" Dad puts down his newspaper and gives us a shifty look.

"We're going round to Ruth's." Clare lies more genuinely than I can manage. "See you later."

Ross is sitting in the front seat with his brother as we walk down the road. I try not to stare, but I can't take my eyes off him. I've never seen such beauty in a man before. His brother is almost as god-like, but his hair is shorter and a few shades darker. I climb into the back of the van with Clare, and feel Ross's eyes looking me up and down as I fumble for my seat. Clare gives him a quick peck on the cheek, and suddenly a knife twists in my heart.

"Evening girls!" Ross catches my eye with a smirk. "How's it going?"

"It's going okay." I try not to smile, but fail miserably. "I've come along hoping to hear a shit-hot band tonight."

"And you shall." Ross looks down my cleavage with interest. "You shall indeed."

"Meet my sister Izzy." Clare runs a finger proprietorially down his arm. "I told her how awesome you are."

"Yeah, I can't help it." Ross chortles with laughter. "Izzy, this is my brother Darryl."

"Hey, beautiful lady…." Darryl starts up the engine. "Every time I look in the rear view mirror I'll see your face."

"Aren't *you* the lucky one!" I roll my eyes heavenwards, but feel inwardly pleased.

The pub is jumping when we get there. Ross and Darryl are joined by Chaz, who plays bass, and Andy, who's on lead guitar, and they all unload the gear out of the van. Clare and I eschew such arduous physical tasks, and idly stand around on the pavement watching them. I cannot help but notice Ross's highly developed musculature; biceps strain whilst he lifts amplifiers, speaker cabinets, and guitars. Darryl is similarly endowed; it's all that drum-bashing I expect. Rhomboids are outlined through his thin shirt, and the quadriceps bulge as he stands up while hoisting an amplifier onto his shoulder from a squatting position. I have the muscle system from *Gray's Anatomy* in my head, and the chance to put theory into practise on such masculine perfection is a welcome one indeed.

Eventually the van is emptied, and Clare and I follow behind the boys like a pair of seasoned groupies. I've been well aware of the undercover glances that Ross has given me, and for Clare's sake I'm trying to ignore the powerful attraction that I have for him. It's strange, because I usually go for the intellectual sorts at medical school; the future professors always seem to hold a strange fascination for me. However, the pull of this rock god cannot be ignored. I'm not sure if he can even spell *intellectual*; he's arty and creative instead. I've never gone for this type before, and by the time he jumps up on stage and grabs his guitar I'm drowning in pheromones.

Clare runs right to the front and looks up at Ross all night, but I stand slightly back in the crowd and lean against a supporting pillar. I obviously look sultry enough because I'm aware that Ross cannot keep his eyes off me. Thankfully Clare has no idea where he's looking, as she's right under his nose. I swallow with the longing to have him inside me.

CHAPTER 7

ROSS

CLARE IS GAZING up at me all night like a cat who's nabbed the last plate of cream, but it's Izzy who is making me lose concentration and play duff notes. Izzy just *exudes* sex. She knows exactly what she's doing; leaning back and fixing me with those dark blue 'come-to-bed' eyes. I've never met somebody so *hot* before. I've tried to get past first post with Clare, and she's always saying she'll go to the doctors and get put on the pill, but she never does. Sad to say I really think she wants to save herself for her wedding night, but after seeing Izzy somehow I no longer *want* to be the one to take first bite of the cherry, so to speak.

I have to wait until Clare goes to the toilet after the first set before I can get Izzy on her own. By then the sweat is pouring out of me, mostly through playing under hot spotlights, but partly through swallowing a couple of uppers from Darryl to keep going, and partly through pure nerves at possibly being rejected. I manage to blurt out to her how nice she looks, and nearly drop dead with shock when she asks if I would like to meet up with her one evening. I can see Clare walking towards me and waving, and tell Izzy quickly that I will wait with the van at the end of her road at about eight o'clock the following night. She nods, smiles, and flashes me one of *those* looks. I know I'm on to a good thing.

The interval goes on longer than usual as some dude collars my brother and will not piss off. I recognise him from a gig we'd done the week before. I make a mental note to ask Darryl why the guy's got him backed into a corner.

Darryl drives both girls home after the gig and I sit in the back of the van with my arm around Clare, feeling like a complete heel for fancying her sister. When we drop them off I give Clare a kiss, and surprisingly for the first time have no hard-on. She throws her arms around my neck and asks when we can meet up again. I don't know quite what to say, and mumble something about ringing her to arrange going out the following weekend. Her lip droops with the knowledge that she will have to wait another whole week to see me again, but at least it gives me seven more days to think of a way to let her down gently.

I watch Izzy walk up the road to her house. She practically *oozes* her way along the pavement, long hair falling like a black curtain down her back. I let out a huge sigh and look at Darryl.

"That's some hot chick." I lean back on the seat and close my eyes.

"You're playing with fire, little brother." Darryl backs the van out into the main road. "If I were you I'd leave both of them alone."

"No can do." I shake my head.

"Then all I can say is *look out*. Clare will be gunning for you as soon as she discovers what's going on."

"I'll sort it." I reply, with a confidence I don't really feel.

Telling Clare I no longer want to see her again is the last thing on my mind as I park Darryl's van in its usual spot well away from the bastard father. My heart is hammering away in my chest and my hands are sweaty. *Will Izzy turn up?* Clare has said that her sister is an intellectual; what does she want with the likes of me?

I don't have to wait long. Dead on eight she opens the front door. I can see she is wearing some sort of thin velvety calf-length skirt and definitely no bra under her top, which is a kind of olive green and a shade lighter than the skirt. On her feet are a pair of strappy sandals.

The old chap starts stiffening at the sight of her. As she climbs into the van the air is suffused with a strong musky perfume. I'm drowning in her; I can hardly breathe.

"You managed to slip away then." I swallow hard and try to concentrate on starting the van.

"Of course; did you think I wouldn't?"

Her smile is teasing. She crosses her legs and looks at me. I put the van in reverse and back around the corner.

"I did have my doubts actually." I return her smile. "Where do you want to go?"

"Somewhere quiet." She touches my leg. "That means very quiet; like, with nobody else around."

The message comes over loud and clear. I rev the van while the cogs in my brain whirr around trying to think of a place I can drive to where we won't be disturbed.

There is no sound outside as I pull into a layby and switch off the engine. I'm sure I've driven almost to Hayling Island before I found a suitable place; a leafy lovers' lane thankfully now under the cover of darkness.

I am breathing fast as I turn to look
at her: "It'll be more comfortable in
the back." "Sure."

She slides the passenger door open and meets me around the back of the van. The doors are already unlocked and we climb inside onto a few cushions I have managed to wangle off Darryl. She lays down, lifts her arms above her head and laces her fingers, resting her head on the palms of her hands and grinning up at me:

"I was hoping for somewhere a little more upmarket."

I need to touch her so badly. I slip my hand under her top and feel her breasts as she arches her back.

"Next time."

I lean over her and take a nipple into my mouth, dark and erect against my lips. When my hand reaches up under her skirt and finds she is not wearing any underwear, I throw any last scruples I might have had left to the wind outside as it rattles through the van's rust-laden chassis.

She is experienced in the ways of sex; with a body like that I knew she would be. I am obviously not her first lover, but as we give intense pleasure to each other for the first time and ride out our mutual frustrations, I am determined to make bloody sure that I am going to be her last.

CHAPTER 8

CLARE

ROSS USUALLY PHONES during the week and lets me know what's happening. It's Friday morning now and I haven't heard from him at all. I catch Mum as she comes home from work, tired and ratty as usual after delivering babies all night. Good God, what a terrible job that must be.

"Have you taken any phone calls from Ross this week?" I feel sure she must have forgotten to tell me he'd phoned.

"No, sorry. Why?" She yawns as she takes off her coat.

"Oh, nothing." I hide my disappointment. "He'll probably phone today then."

But he doesn't. I find myself hanging about in the hallway by the telephone in case Izzy answers his call by mistake, although she seems to sleep in later and later these days; I don't know how she's going to get up early for her studies when term starts again. I heard her creeping in late a couple of evenings this week, but I don't know where she's been. She was quite chatty when she first came home, but lately she's kept very much to herself.

I can't concern myself too much with Izzy at the moment; it's Ross I'm worried about. Why hasn't he phoned me? I can't go a fortnight without seeing him! I know he uses a public phone box to call me because his parents don't have a phone, but surely there must be at least one phone in his neighbourhood that hasn't been vandalised?

Izzy finds me sitting on the telephone seat eating a lunchtime sandwich as she comes downstairs in her pyjamas. I smile at her but she avoids looking at me:

"Has Ross called here, do you know?" I try and catch her eye.

"Er….no, I don't think so."

Izzy carries on through to the kitchen, and not for the first time I wonder why she's suddenly so moody. I follow her down the hallway and deposit my plate in the sink.

"What's up?"

I stare at her impatiently, waiting for an answer. She stands at the kettle in silence, and takes her time making a cup of coffee. Finally with a sigh she finishes stirring in some sugar and takes a sip.

"Look; I think you ought to know something."

My stomach takes a sudden lurch at the tone of her voice. I know that whatever she's going to say will not be at all to my advantage. I swallow nervously and my voice comes out as a kind of bleat.

"What?"

"There's no easy way to tell you this, but….me and Ross; we're an item."

My legs suddenly turn to jelly, and I run to sit down.   I cannot quite believe what I have just heard, and for a brief moment wonder if I have been mistaken.

"What did you say?"

Izzy puts her cup of coffee on the workbench and comes over towards me, putting an arm around my shoulder.

"I just hate to have to be the one to tell you this, but I don't think Ross can bring himself to say anything. We just clicked that night at the gig; I'm so sorry, but Ross and I….well…..we wanted each other and we made love; again I'm sorry. I feel like a complete heel, but I can't stop the feelings I have for him, nor he for me."

My whole world falls apart in an instant. The boy whom I imagined sharing the rest of my life with and my sister, who if anything should be on my side through thick and thin, have betrayed me. I purposely try and push the mental image away of them lying naked together and stand up.

"Don't touch me! How could you do this?" I sob bitterly and run to the door, taking one last look over my shoulder at Izzy. "Why don't you go back to London and leave us alone? Everything was fine until you came along!"

"I'm not going back to London." Izzy sat down in the chair I had just vacated and looked at the floor. "I'm staying here with Ross. I'm going to get a job instead."

"Well, that's just fucking fine!" My voice breaks like an adolescent schoolboy's. "Thanks for ruining my life! I hope the two of you rot in hell!"

I manage to lock my bedroom door before I let the tears cascade down my cheeks. I fling myself face down on my bed and wail bitterly into my pillow. I cannot see how I can go on; my sister has had sex with the love of my life, and now

Dad will be impossible to live with once he knows that Izzy has given up on her medical studies. I can foresee no joy at all for years.

I hear Izzy's footsteps hesitate at my door but then go on to the bathroom. At this precise moment in time I hate my sister with a fury that I never knew existed. As for Ross; what kind of man was he to play with my emotions like this?

When the tears cease falling it comes to me in a flash why Ross chose Izzy over me. One word springs to mind; *sex*. By stupidly wanting to save myself for our wedding night I have inadvertently pushed Ross into Izzy's arms through sheer sexual frustration. He does not, *cannot* really love *her*; I know that as soon as we make love he will realise it as well. It now dawns crystal clear to me what I have to do.

I can hear Izzy running a bath. Quietly I creep downstairs and reach under the telephone table for the Yellow Pages, quickly searching through the doctors' surgeries until I find the number for our one. It takes but a moment to book an appointment that will change the course of my life forever and bring Ross running back to me.

CHAPTER 9

MARIAN

I WISH CLARE had never met that boy. The calm order of
our house has been turned totally upside down. Clare's misery
is absolute, and no matter how Donald rants and raves he
cannot persuade Isabel to change her mind. She has this
preposterous notion of giving up three years of studies at
medical school and taking a job stacking shelves or some
other awful occupation just to be near him. She is adamant
that she will not return to London in a fortnight, but Donald
will not cancel her digs; he shouts at her that she is going
back to her studies, but she shakes her head defiantly and
informs him she is not.

My girls are now strangers to me and to each other. The
silence in our house is oppressive, and is only broken by
Donald's raised voice when Isabel strays into his line of
vision. I tell him he is driving her away, but he is intent on his
own mission of dominating his daughters and making them
obey his every command. It might have worked when they

were small, but he fails to understand that they are now grown women.

I saw the contraceptive pills which Clare left out of her bedside cabinet by mistake that one time. She's obviously changed her mind about saving herself for her wedding night, and it saddens me immensely to think that the boy may now be fornicating with not only one, but both of my daughters. I know Clare is hanging around the pubs where his band has gigs, and I worry about venereal disease; who knows just how many people he has had sex with?

Both girls keep their own counsel, and neither one shares any gossip with me or with each other like they used to do. The atmosphere at home can be likened to a powder keg waiting to explode.

Tonight the explosion takes place at dinner. Clare now eats her meals in her room to avoid Isabel, and so it is just three of us at the table. Isabel plays her trump card and announces that she is going to live with the boy and his parents. She has some deluded notion that he's going to be a rock star, and says the band have been spotted by a talent scout. Apparently she has found some dead-end office job in town, near to the art college. Donald throws down his knife and fork without even finishing his meal and drives off somewhere to try and cool down and come to terms with it all. Isabel weeps, kisses me and apologises profusely, but it seems that she cannot live without *the boy*.

She packs and has gone off with him in the van before Donald returns. I knock on Clare's bedroom door and prepare to break the news.

"Clare; may I come in?" I listen intently for an answer. There is none.

The door is unlocked, and I enter tentatively. I look at my youngest daughter lying passively on the bed, dishevelled and distraught, and want to wrap her in my arms and tell her that everything is alright like I used to do when she was a little girl, only this time I know that she must prepare for more sorrow.

"Isabel has moved out, darling." I sit on the bed and stroke her head. "It's for the best, I think."

A pent-up tornado hurls itself at me.

"I loved him, Mum! I really loved him!" She sobs into my shoulder. "But he doesn't want me! He only wants *her!*"

"You are young and pretty; you have plenty of time to find somebody who *really* loves you." I emphasise the *really*, as I suspect Ross's interest was purely sexual. "Before long you would have forgotten all about him, I'm sure."

I hold her tight while she rails against the entire male sex. I can tell she is devastated that all her womanly charms and wiles have been unsuccessful; it now appears that Ross and Isabel are a couple and that Clare will have to get used to the idea.

I learn that she is indeed taking the contraceptive pill, initially for the reason of luring Ross back from Isabel, but now also in order to lose a worrisome virginity should the chance present itself. I gently tell her to be in no hurry to become a woman; it is always best that intimacy occurs within a loving marriage. She tells me I am old-fashioned and behind the times. I sigh and hold my baby closer, wishing she was five years old again, and also wanting to somehow encircle her broken heart with an impenetrable wall.

It is a mother's lot to worry. I am anxious that she does

not go and sleep with the first boy who shows any interest. Living for forty six years has given me great insight into the male psyche; if Donald is anything to go by it is primarily for sex without love to spread the seed far and wide, which is the exact opposite of Clare's needs. She is sensitive and yearns to be loved; giving herself out of desperation to whomever can only bring her more pain and sorrow.

Yes, I am resigned to Donald's affairs. There are little signs I can pick up on to tell me if another fanciable patient or attractive member of staff has appeared on the scene; new clothes in the wardrobe, a haircut, expensive aftershave, erratic working hours, presents to assuage his guilt, and a distance in the bedroom, which after all these years is now not necessarily a bad thing as I approach the menopause. However, it leaves me with growing feelings of worthlessness and depression, the latter sometimes being very hard to shift.

Donald has a kind of haunted look this week; the shock of having to cancel Isabel's digs and course studies brought the stark reality of her decision home to him. He has stopped shouting, but instead is uncommunicative and now rather resigned to the fact that all the hopes and dreams he had for his eldest daughter have been dashed. I try to tell him that our girls are old enough to make their own life choices, and that it is our duty as parents to encourage them in ways which will make them happy. I always had my doubts as to whether Isabel really wanted to become a doctor, or if she was just acting out her father's wishes. Actually, if truth be told, I rather lean towards the latter.

Isabel phoned yesterday evening to inform us that she has managed to secure a post as an Exams Clerk at the art college where Ross is studying. She can begin her new job straight away, and is happier than she has ever been now that the stress of forcing herself to do something she was not enjoying has disappeared. All I can do is be glad that she has found joy in her life. Donald cannot bring himself to speak to her, and passes the telephone over to me the minute he hears her voice at the other end.

I question her endlessly, greedy for information. She tells me that she is happy with Ross, and that they are very much in love. Apparently his parents are thrilled to bits with her. They are not very well off, but are kind and thoughtful and are happy to let her live at their home until she and Ross can afford a flat of their own. She will pay Donna, Ross's mother, part of her wages for her keep.

Isabel asks after Clare, and I tell her that unfortunately her sister is heartbroken and still no longer wishes to speak to her. There is a silence whilst Isabel digests this information, and I am sadly aware of sobbing at the other end of the phone. There is nothing I can do or say to ease the situation, and eventually I say goodbye and replace the receiver with a heavy heart. I am tired.

CHAPTER 10

CLARE

IT'S GOOD TO be at University. The summer was so disastrous; the relief to have something to do to take my mind off Ross can only be beneficial for me in the long run. Studying English leaves me plenty of time to socialise, and I've become a bit of a party animal. The personality change pleases me; I've shaken off all those fuddy-duddy warnings my mother gave out, and have thrown myself headlong into the social scene.

I met Tony Bartholomew, a second year Chemistry student, at a party soon after the term began, and finally with a certain amount of pain and embarrassment I lost my virginity. Tony thinks it's a great hoot that I was still a virgin at 19, and we spend as much time as we can at his digs finding out what pleases each other. I'm not sure how many girlfriends Tony's had, and I don't like to ask, but he says he loves me. However, unfortunately I don't know if I love him or not; he's fun to be around and we have good sex, but he's not Ross.

Ross. He will always be my first love and the one that got away. I often laugh at myself though, for being so prim and proper and saving it all up for my wedding night. Once you've had sex, it's not such a big deal after all. The thought of stripping naked in front of a man initially scared me, but basically I don't know why I made such a big thing of it.

My mother gives me little snippets of information that Izzy passes on to her, and I try to act noncommittal as I listen, but inwardly I'm grasping at anything that might tell me that their romance is over. Apparently Izzy's enjoying her job at the college, and Ross is out every night with the band trying to earn some money. I cannot believe that my sister is no longer going to be a doctor. For so long it was taken for granted that she was the brains of the family, and now it is second best Clare who is on course to have the profession instead. *My my, how the cookie crumbles.* Mum tells me that Izzy is apparently desperate to get back in my good books, but as far as I'm concerned she can trot off to hell in a handcart.

It's nearly Christmas, and I more or less live at Tony's digs now, sharing his single bed and generally being accepted as his girlfriend. I take turns to cook with the other five students in the house, and they never let on to the landlord that there's an extra body not paying any rent. To be honest I don't really like going home; Dad is a shadow of his former self, and Mum frets and fusses around trying to make him happy. I think he had this pipe dream where Izzy followed him and specialised in Dermatology, but I could never see my sister looking at somebody's spots and moles all day long anyway. When she gave up her studies it knocked the stuffing out of him, and I can't bear to see him as he is now. My sister has a lot to answer for.

When I go back home for Christmas lunch I need to plan it so that I don't bump into her. Tony will be going home to his parents who live in Oxford, and I don't fancy staying in the student house all on my own. Even worse is the fact that she may bring Ross with her just to spite me; if she did I just couldn't bear it. Dad apparently has relented over Ross in order not to lose Izzy, and so I will need to phone Mum and find out what time they will be arriving on Christmas Day. What I would have liked is to have been invited to Tony's parents' house, but unfortunately no invite has materialised.

Tony gives me a small square-shaped present before he leaves for Oxford, and asks me to open it even though it's not quite Christmas Eve. I'm surprised to find a little eternity ring sitting in a blue velvet box. He must have saved up all his wages from working evenings at the Wimpy Bar to buy it. I am touched; it's a lovely gift and he puts it on the third finger of my right hand, kisses me, and tells me again that he loves me. I cling to him and wish he was Ross. He puts his arms around me and whispers into my ear.

"Someday if you're agreeable, I'll buy you an engagement ring as well."

I'm not sure how to respond. I just squeeze him and enjoy the warmth from his body. The other students have all gone home for Christmas, and we have the house to ourselves. Just for once we light some candles and make love on the fake fur rug in the front room, bringing down Tony's duvet to snuggle under afterwards to keep warm.

I phone Mum, who tells me that Izzy and Ross will be having Christmas Day lunch with Donna and Steve, and then Izzy will make a visit home late afternoon to stay for supper and open presents. I quickly work out that I will have to visit Christmas Eve, stay for lunch the next day, and then rush back to the student flat until she goes.

I make the pilgrimage home and lay wide awake in my old bedroom on Christmas Eve, now unused to sleeping without Tony's body wrapped around me. The house is cheerless. Mum has gone to town with the decorations again, but an all-pervading sadness is hard to ignore.

Mum comes in for an early Christmas morning chat like she always used to do. I'm still awake and reading one of my old Nancy Drew mysteries, trying to conjure up the long-lost excitement of Christmases past. Mum plonks herself on the end of my bed and sighs. She looks tired and worn out.

"I'm afraid Izzy won't come here today without Ross. She says they're a couple now, and Dad either gets both of them or none at all."

"It's okay, Mum. If you could give me a lift back to Tony's flat after lunch, I'd be very grateful. There'll be no taxis around, and if there are, the rates will be extortionate."

"Of course I will, and I'll bring you back later on. It's just that I wondered…..well…..if you could stay and maybe make friends again?"

Mum looks at me hopefully but I put the book down and shake my head:

"No way. Sorry, but too much has happened, and now I need to be someplace where she isn't."

"I understand." Mum looks sadder than ever. "Perhaps with time….."

I shake my head again. The pain of losing Ross is still too raw.

"Sorry; she can't have everything her own way."

I give Mum a hug, climb out of bed, and decide to make the most of my brief stay at home.

"Come on; let's get Dad up and open our presents. It is Christmas after all."

CHAPTER 11

DONALD

I TRY NOT to think of all the money, time and effort that has been invested in the girls' education, especially Isabel's. It's almost too much to bear for a father to find out that his daughter, who possesses the ability to pass every medical exam put in front of her, is now a run-of-the-mill office clerk instead.

We had such high hopes for Isabel. From a very early age she was streets ahead of all her contemporaries. Clare is intelligent enough, but Isabel *shines*. Marian has had no success in persuading her to change her mind and continue with her studies. Isabel seems to have lost her head completely to that ghastly boy, whom I will struggle dreadfully to be civil to at the supper table today. He has caused such a rift in our family which I fear can never be healed. We are torn; broken apart.

Clare and Marian will want to open presents soon, so I am going to get out of bed and take as long as I can in the bathroom; the sooner Christmas is over with the better. Today has such abnormally high expectations, which this year alas we cannot live up to. The light of my life has ceased to shine, and to be quite honest I would prefer it if Isabel and the wretched boy would stay away. Clare feels that she must leave the house while they're here, but somehow I think it should be the other way around; I have nothing left to say to Isabel now.

I keep a watch through the blinds, and see him walking up the garden path with my daughter. His hair flows past his shoulders and resembles a girl's. By the look of him he's obviously never owned a suit in his life; he's wearing some sort of ribbed jumper, well-worn jeans, and cowboy-like boots with pointed toes. Isabel is simpering up at him as though he's some kind of demi-god. If I knew I would not get caught, nothing would give me greater pleasure than to apply firm pressure to his hyoid bone.......

Isabel is keeping up some kind of manic conversation as Marian dishes up some cold turkey with Bubble & Squeak. The boy stays silent and catches my eye every now and then. We pull crackers and I open one of the less expensive bottles of wine; the bastard will never know the difference anyway. Trite and meaningless, Isabel waffles on until I hear something that causes me to look up at her in shock and horror.

"So I'll carry on working until the beginning of July probably; the baby is due around the fifteenth of August."

The food is tasteless and sticks like glue to the back of my throat. I cough and manage to swallow a chunk of turkey.

"What did you say?" A rage wells up inside me that I'm

trying very hard to contain.

"I'm pregnant, Dad. We found out a couple of days ago. Be happy for us."

The boy looks down at the carpet, with an expression likened to that of somebody who has just been informed he has acquired a dose of the pox. I see Isabel has taken hold of his hand, while Marian is waving a serviette about in the air and gushing out congratulatory words that are somehow falling flat. As for myself, I can no longer pretend that everything is hunky-dory.

"Well, now you seem to have ruined your life completely!" The anger has taken over; I throw down my knife and fork and stand up. "Isn't it enough that you've thrown in your medical studies to be with this imbecile? What next? I suppose you want me to keep the three of you as well!"

I can no longer bear to be in the same room as the boy. As I turn for the door he stands up and blocks my exit. My hands ball into fists as he meets me eye to eye.

"No, Sir." His voice is quiet but firm. "Okay, I'm still a student at the art college, but my band was recently spotted by a talent scout when we played a gig at the Wig and Pen. We're now in the middle of negotiating a record contract with Perseid Records. Fortunately, we seem to be in the position of being all set to make more money than you've ever seen in your entire life."

My misery is complete. Not only has this pie-in-the-sky godawful wailing musician broken my youngest daughter's heart, my eldest daughter, formerly a brilliant medical student but now a pregnant groupie, is destined to follow behind him for the rest of her natural life, no doubt producing a flock of flower-bedecked bohemian, long-haired children with depressing regularity and turning into some kind of all–encompassing earth mother in a kaftan, attending to everyone's needs but her own.

"I'll believe that when I see it." I match his stare and do not back away.

"Believe it. The contract will be signed as soon as the lawyer's finished looking it over."

The long-haired layabout nods to confirm his statement. I push past him, eager to be gone from the whole charade. He has as much chance of making it big in the music industry as a pork chop has of getting inside a synagogue.

The relief of closing the bedroom door and letting them all get on with it downstairs is overwhelming. When I eventually hear the brother outside with the van, I make sure Isabel and the boy get in it before I go back downstairs.

Marian is washing up the supper things. I grab a tea towel.

"One of us needs to go and pick up Clare now that they've gone." Unsmiling, she hands me a glass lid to wipe.

"I'll go. Be prepared for more tears when she gets back; I'll tell her about the pregnancy." I sigh at the unpleasant task ahead. "Will they get married?"

"Who knows?" Marian shrugs. "They don't seem to think a piece of paper saying that they're married is going to change the way they feel about each other."

"Great; now my grandchild will be a bastard, just like its father." I sigh bitterly, weighed down with untold grief.

CHAPTER 12

CLARE

I REALISE NOW I will never win Ross back and that I have to move on. I phoned Mum yesterday, who told me that Izzy came round to see them. Apparently she is 'radiant', and only has about another four months to go before the baby is born. I haven't seen her since well before Christmas, and I still have no intention of doing so. The thought of them together as a cosy little family eats me up inside. I tend not to go home very much now in case she's there. To make it worse, Ross and the band signed the Perseid Records' contract at the end of January, and the band have a few big support gigs planned. I tear up when I think that it could have been me waiting in the wings backstage for Ross. Izzy apparently even got Ross to change the band's name as soon as she felt the baby move; they're now called 'Kick'.

I've made a new set of friends at the university. Ethan and his girlfriend Rhiann were friends of Tony's to start with, but they've included me in their circle now that we're a couple. Damon and Cathy are more on my wavelength though; Ethan drinks too much, and is often trolleyed in the middle of the afternoon. I think possibly he has that sort of addictive personality; he can't just have one pint of beer, he needs to drink the whole barrel.

I still wear Tony's ring, and almost every day he asks me about getting engaged, but I tell him I'm too young to be thinking about that yet. He tells me he will never give up asking. I'm fond of him, but it's not like that rush of emotion I felt with Ross. No other boys ever ask me out, and that's because they know I'm with Tony. I often feel I'm suffocating in his love, and sometimes want to leap out of the student flat and keep on running. I know he loves me desperately, and it's nice to feel loved, but I'm beginning to feel I hooked up with Tony for the worst possible reasons; to get away from home and my sister, and to prove to everyone that at least one other person finds me attractive.

Tony seems to have a possessive streak that is coming more and more to the fore the longer I remain with him. He now likes us to spend cosy evenings in his room at the flat, just the two of us. The other five students are all male, and he's starting to go on about them looking at me or of me noticing them. I have to speak to them sometimes as it would be rude to ignore them, since we are all living in the same house, but the sulking I have had to put up with recently from Tony is starting to irritate. I find myself more drawn to Damon these days. He's taller than Ross, quite fair-haired, and rather muscly. Dad would like him I think, but of course there's no way I can become closer to Damon all the while he's with Cathy.

The Easter holidays will soon be upon us, and Mum and Dad are expecting Tony and me to come home on Easter Sunday for lunch. No doubt the pregnant sister will put in an appearance at some point; I will have to check with Mum as to when the coast is clear. I don't want to see evidence of Izzy and Ross's lovemaking parading in front of me, and I don't want to see any photos of the baby when it arrives either. Mum to my mind is not looking very well, but she can hardly hide her excitement at becoming a grandmother; it's pathetic. She's buying up piles of baby clothes, knitting cardigans, and generally acting as if the baby's going to be the most important person in the whole world.

When I phoned Mum yesterday to check on arrival times, the bottom dropped out of my world. She's bubbling over with joy that Ross has decided to make an honest woman of Izzy, and the registry office wedding is set for a Friday afternoon at the end of May. Izzy will be six months' pregnant; she'll have to buy a large bouquet to cover up the bump. The council has given them a maisonette, and Ross is making enough money to pay the rent now he's getting some larger gigs with Kick.

I'll just probably go to Uni as normal on the day of the wedding. Mum says she has no intention of missing it, and nothing is going to keep her away. Well, there I'm afraid our paths diverge…..nothing, absolutely nothing, is going to make me attend.

I think Mum and Dad feel a bit guilty about their treatment of Ross, which has the advantage of them almost falling over backwards to be nice to Tony. Dad is positively sycophantic when Tony steps through the door, and of course Tony is lapping it up. He's already made it clear to them that he wants to marry me, and it seems they've said and done everything to agree with him except march me down the aisle. I'm suffocating and under pressure to get engaged. I want to continue my studies and become a teacher, but Tony doesn't want me to work if we get married. He's already set to start out on the first rung of the ladder to eventually become a research scientist, and he takes his finals in June. If he can work, why can't I? Why doesn't *he* give up work if we get married? The bloody cheek of it!

It's no good. I look at Tony as we sit down for the traditional Easter turkey dinner, and I know that I don't want to live under his stifling, smothering presence anymore. I realise I'm going to have to cause another upset in the family by ditching Tony and moving back home. I'll be 20 at the beginning of August, and I *know* I could not bear a life chained to the kitchen sink, frightened to speak to anybody male in case I caused trouble, and weighed down with a string of babies pulling at my womb and my apron. I'm sinking and I need Ross to rescue me, but as far as he's concerned I might as well drown.

So much for my vow to remain a virgin until my wedding night. Now I'm soiled along with the rest of them. I'm starting to think that Mum might have had something when she told me that men like to marry a virgin because they don't like being compared to previous lovers. Well, girls are people too; in my opinion they also don't like to think their man has been with countless other women. I'd like to marry a virgin as well, but I can't see it happening somehow.

I wonder who will want me now?

CHAPTER 13

IZZY

I ZIP UP my wedding dress and feel like a beached whale. The washboard stomach has long gone, and I now have what resembles a sack of potatoes around my middle. I turn sideways in Mum's mirror, and my new matronly figure causes one depressing thought to fly through my head: *just zip me up and call me King Edward...*

This wasn't the kind of wedding that I had envisioned for myself; six months up the duff and looking like a female version of Demis Roussos. Ross says I still turn him on, but I have to turn the light out now when we make love.

Mum is going to do my make-up. I don't really care what I look like though; it's impossible to look sexy with a huge stomach sticking out the front. Sometimes I wonder how Jeff and the other guys are getting on at medical school and whether I did the right thing in leaving, but it's too late to change my mind now. Ross is away with the band quite a lot, and most days I'm lumbering about the house bored witless.

There's no way I'd want to sleep on the tour bus at the moment; Ross has enough on his plate trying to please the record company, and I know he wouldn't want a pregnant wife complaining about her aches and pains adding to his problems.

I'm so proud of him. The band are doing really well, and their manager has sorted out some really great support gigs. Fans are starting to follow them from gig to gig, and the music industry is definitely sitting up and taking notice. It would be even better if Ross didn't smoke so much cannabis, but I suppose it keeps him calm.

Please God we will soon be able to move out of the awful hole where we're living now. I can't go back home to Mum and Dad when Ross is away because Clare's there in the evenings and the atmosphere is terrible. I've driven my sister away, and now I've got to pay the price.

I can hear them all downstairs; Mum, Aunt Sally, Aunt Linda, and the cousins. I know they're talking about me; *the pregnant bride having a shotgun wedding*. However, Ross and I made the decision together to marry without any outside interference. I don't think his parents were too keen on the idea though, as they consider he's too young. It goes without saying that my dad is dead set against me marrying Ross, and has refused to go to the wedding, along with Clare. Apparently Dad drove Clare to Uni this morning and then went off to the hospital, just like any other working day, and so I was able to sneak round to the house and be with Mum. Out of my immediate family only Mum is going to the wedding, and it makes me sad. I don't know if it's the pregnancy hormones or not, but at the moment all I want to do is cry. I'm not even looking much forward to the baby coming.

I can hear Mum coming upstairs. She seems slower than usual, and when she opens the door I can see that she's lost weight. I haven't seen her for a few weeks. I take a second glance, and realise that under her fancy new hat and dress she really looks quite under the weather.

"Are you okay, Mum?" I turn from the mirror and smile at her.

"Just a bit tired, having to run around after Sally. I've put her in your old bedroom; thank goodness she's going home tomorrow."

Mum even seems a bit breathless after climbing the stairs, which is unusual.

"Take it easy; you look knackered." I walk over and give her a hug. "Let Sally run around after you."

"I'll be okay." Mum returns the hug. "Let's get you made up; there's not much time left."

Uncle Stan is going to drive me there and give me away. He's decorated his silver grey Capri with ribbons and bows, and it gleams in the sunshine. The aunts and cousins all make the required noises of appreciation when Mum and I go downstairs, but it's all I can do to be civil to them. I just want to get today over with; the registrar will be looking at my stomach, and I'll look huge in all the photos. I've come to the conclusion that to get married when I am six months' pregnant is a really, really bad idea.

I assume everyone's already inside when Stan and I arrive

at the registry office. The pavement outside is empty, and there's just someone's used toffee wrappers blowing about on the pavement. I pick up my bouquet of red roses and place them strategically over the bump.

"You look lovely." Uncle Stan can lie for England. He locks the car and holds out his arm.

"I look like the side of a frigging house." I mumble and slip my arm through his. "Thanks for doing this though."

"My pleasure; Aunt Linda and your mum have had a good old natter as well. We haven't seen you all for ages."

"Yeah; it's usually only at weddings and funerals when our families meet up, isn't it?"

As I walk down the aisle with Stan to some godawful music, the rest of the band and their girlfriends seated at the back start to clap. I can't help but smile. None of them are dressed for a wedding; Chaz still has the Led Zeppelin t-shirt on that he wore to Kick's last gig, and I'm sure Andy and his girlfriend are stoned.

Ross, seated down the front with Darryl, turns around to look at me. Suddenly I *know* the reason why I'm going through all this crap. I just happen to be marrying the most beautiful man I've ever seen in my whole life; a man who is a gifted songwriter and singer, and who the whole world is going to know about before too long. I hold the roses close to me and grin at my man, looking incongruous and decidedly uncomfortable as he stands there in a grey Marks & Spencer's pinstripe suit, cream-coloured shirt and kipper tie. The congregation are blissfully unaware that he's probably standing there with a stash of weed in his inside pocket for later. He winks back at me, and then turns around again to face the registrar.

A registry office wedding is a bit like being on a conveyor belt; the next couple are in the waiting room ready to come in as soon as you've tied the knot and have escaped to the pub for a couple of rounds of ham sandwiches and a pint of beer. I was just thankful to get the whole process over with, pose for the photos, and get the hell out of there.

There's no money for a honeymoon. Mum used some of her savings to pay for the pub food, but Dad has held off handing over the money he'd been putting away for years. Deep joy; so now it looks as though Clare and Tony will get a double amount. Never mind; *I'm* the one who has Ross!

CHAPTER 14

MARIAN

I THOUGHT IT was all the build-up to the wedding and organising everything that was making me feel tired, but the dreadful fatigue is still here a month later. However, if truth be told I know I've been feeling ill for absolutely ages before the wedding, but I can't deny it any longer. All I feel like doing is curling up in bed and sleeping. I keep having to take sick days at work, which makes me feel guilty as then the other midwives have to work doubly hard to cover for my absence. I haven't said anything to Donald, but he found me asleep on the settee when he came home from work yesterday, and it was only four o'clock in the afternoon. I've lost a stone in weight because I feel sick and have no appetite, and my leg muscles scream at me if I try and walk upstairs. Donald compliments me on my new size 12 dress, but with all the medical training I've had I know I shall have to go to the GP to find out why I'm feeling so drowsy and weak.

Clare asks me if I'm okay, but Donald carries on as usual,

lost in his own little world. They always say doctors' families never get the sympathy and bedside manner if they're ill that their patients receive, and I think that's true. I'm sure my husband wouldn't notice if I shrivel away to nothing.

I make the phone call. Luckily Donald has an evening clinic on Mondays and I can visit the doctor's surgery without him knowing. I drive down as my legs ache too much, and I sit in the waiting room surrounded by old people with coughs and mothers with screaming toddlers. The GP takes one look at me and organises urine and blood tests. He wonders if I have a kidney infection. He checks my ankles, which are a bit swollen, and asks me to come back tomorrow evening for the results.

Donald isn't working tomorrow, and so I'll have to tell him where I'm going. I'm sure all the symptoms are nothing to worry about though; it's either the menopause or I'm just a little run down.

Donald insists on accompanying me to the surgery. All the GP's know him, so perhaps it's not a bad thing; at least I know I'll probably get some preferential treatment. I watch him casting his professional eye over me, and I start to panic in case it's cancer or something dire. I want to live to see my grandchild grow up; Isabel only has another 2 months to go, and she'll need me on hand to help when the baby's born. She's been on at me for ages to find out what the matter is, but I suppose I've been in denial that there's anything wrong with me.

My heart is pounding as I sit down with Donald and face

the GP. He tells me that the results show my kidneys are not functioning as they should. He breaks the news that I will shortly have to go into hospital for tests. I feel relieved that at least it's probably not cancer, but now I will need to tell Isabel and Clare. Isabel I'll talk to when she comes to visit next, but no doubt Clare will already be home. She doesn't seem to want to stay at Tony's place so often now, and has made a new set of friends. I'm happy that she's blossoming at last.

The hospital phone me the very next day and say they have a bed ready in the renal ward. I can't believe this is all happening to *me*. Clare goes off to University with a worried look on her face, but I tell her the short stay is only for tests and that I will be home soon. Donald finds a junior to take his clinic and comes with me when I am admitted, refusing to leave when I'm examined and generally being his usual assertive self even though he has no jurisdiction in this part of the hospital. I am worried about what the tests are going to show, but try and stay cheerful in front of Donald.

There seems to be a battery of blood tests, x-rays, and urine tests set up for me. The phlebotomists are cheery as they stick needles in my arm and talk about the weather, but I can't seem to match their bonhomie with my own. I'm scared stiff, and when Donald goes off to pick Clare up from Uni I have a little cry in the toilet all by myself.

Mr Carter-Brown is the renal surgeon, and is followed into the ward by a team of juniors and medical students when he makes his rounds. I feel a momentary pang of regret that Isabel will never be a part of either his or any other consultant's team, but quickly put it to the back of my mind when he tells me the x-rays have shown that I was born with only one kidney, and that the combined result of all the blood and urine tests are pointing towards the one remaining kidney being in a state of end-stage failure. I learn to my horror that I need immediate dialysis and eventually will need to have a transplant. He adds in almost as an afterthought that I have a rare blood group, which will probably increase my waiting time for a new kidney unless a suitable donor from the immediate family can be found. I now need to alter my diet to cut out salt, potassium and phosphorous, and drink less as apparently my urine output is poor. I need to see the dietitian to get a list of foods I must avoid.

I can't seem to take it all in; the surgeon's words swim round and round in my head. I had no idea that I was born with only one kidney. My adoptive parents obviously never knew, as nothing was ever said to me during their lifetime, and I can only assume that perhaps my birth mother or father also suffered with kidney disease. Who knows? It is a grey area; I always looked upon Mum and Dad as my parents, but of course I was not biologically related to either of them whatsoever.

When Donald and Clare come in to see me I can't help but break down in tears. I realise I am not well enough to work at the moment, and feel suddenly useless and a drain on my family. No wonder Donald always has a mistress on the go. What use am I?

I don't know what to do.

CHAPTER 15

IZZY

I HAD A bit of a shock today when I lumbered round to see Mum. She wanted to keep the news from me, but it seems she is now having regular dialysis for kidney failure. She looks terrible, and has to go for treatment three times a week. When I hug her I realise how much weight she has lost. She says she feels sick a lot of the time, but the dialysis is helping with that, although it gives her increased muscle pains. I try and hide my worry at the sight of her, and mention a thought that I cannot put off no matter how I try:

"What about a transplant?"

Mum shakes her head:

"Clare's been tested, but she has Dad's blood group, and so it's no match I'm afraid. Trust me to have a rare blood type; it could be ages before a donor is found."

The unspoken plea is there, but I'm filled with horror at the thought of it. I am seven months' pregnant and in no state to undergo surgery, even if one of my kidneys *is* a match for Mum. If I remember from med school, it's even possible for a child to take its grandparents' blood group instead. I have no idea who Mum's real parents or grandparents were, as she always told Clare and I from a very early age that she was adopted. I sigh inwardly as I realise that to keep her alive and well it'll probably be all down to me:

"I'm happy to be tested."

I hope the lie sounds convincing. Mum nods and thanks me for the offer, but she is steadfastly against me having an anaesthetic or any surgery while I am pregnant or breastfeeding. I hug her in relief and breathe easier; it seems in my 'delicate' condition I am spared surgery for the moment.

The relief on Ross's face is evident as I let him know what's happening about Mum, and that for the moment all I'm going to do is be tested for a match. The band are halfway through a UK tour supporting *Orange Transporter*, and he's managed to slip away for the weekend. He's buzzing like never before; to tour with a famous band is one thing and to sit with Eddie and Mick and talk about song lyrics is a dream come true, but now *Kick* are gathering a sizeable fan base of their own. My husband is on cloud nine, and informs me with great delight that we can afford for a phone and an answering machine to be fitted in the house. He tells me to go ahead and organise it, and that he will be back in a month when the tour comes to an end. I cannot wait to have him home again.

I welcome the phone's installation and the chance to speak to Mum on a daily basis. It's also a comfort to know that I can phone for an ambulance if the baby starts to arrive before its due date. Ross doesn't think he can take being in the labour room, and to be quite honest I'd rather be somewhere else instead too, but hey, perhaps they can knock me out.

Mum continues to deteriorate despite four hours of dialysis three times a week. She is a horrible yellowy-grey colour, and can hardly walk due to muscle pain. With great trepidation I undergo the necessary blood test, but discover that I have the same blood group as Dad and Clare, A positive, whereas Mum is O negative, and can only receive a kidney from an O negative donor, about 8% of the population. Ross can hardly hide his relief when he calls me from Newcastle and I update him with the news; I must admit I was not looking forward to the painful surgery and having to lose a vital part of my body. Poor Mum has given up her job now, and to me she looks as though she is living on borrowed time, although she has been told that the average life expectancy on dialysis is 5 – 10 years. She must have been in denial of her illness, struggling to work for as long as she could, and wanting to live a normal life. If only she had sought treatment earlier. Every day I wait to hear that a kidney has become available for her, but with the knowledge of her rare blood group I realise I have a better chance of flying to the moon.

I miss my sister. Sometimes when I call Mum Clare answers the phone, but hands it over straight away. I want us to be friends again, but somehow I know that will never be. I chose Ross over her, and she is going to punish me for it for the rest of my life. Mum tells me that Clare doesn't want me to know anything about what's going on in her life, and so all I can talk about on the phone to Mum is her illness or my pregnancy. It's as though my sister never existed. My baby will never know an aunt, uncle or cousins on my side of the family. I am in despair.

Ross comes home for the last month of my pregnancy. It's so wonderful to have him back. He is exhausted and has lost weight through hauling amps, speaker cabinets and guitars in and out of the trailer from gig to gig, but his eyes are bright when he shows me a copy of the New Musical Express. *Kick* have their photos and an article about them on the third page. I realise with a growing excitement that through their tour with *Orange Transporter* my husband and the other band members have become minor celebrities overnight. A second tour is planned for September; this time with the Irish rockers *Squiffey*. I ask Ross what the bands get up to when they're not playing, but he says mysteriously that what goes on tour stays on tour. I worry about drugs, but it's no use asking him anything. I look down at my swollen stomach and decide it's best not to know.

I find myself frantically cleaning the house as the time draws nearer to the birth. Ross thinks I have gone crazy, especially when he sees me knitting, and I realise I am doing the age-old thing of feathering my nest. We seem to have quite a bit of money to live on from the tour, and it's wonderful to have my husband at home with me at such an important time in our lives. He has bought a second-hand car; one of those Triumph sporty jobs with the big bonnet and small boot. I look at it and wonder how on earth we're going to get a pushchair in the back, but I keep quiet as I don't want to burst his bubble. He's riding high at the moment, enjoying doing the macho provider rock star thing. With his thick, blond hair falling down his back he certainly looks the part, but all I can think of is how many other women he might have had sex with in the back of the tour bus.

CHAPTER 16

MARIAN

A LIGHT IN the bleak darkness of kidney failure; my little granddaughter was born yesterday, Monday 2nd August, the day before Clare's birthday. Clare does not want to know, and so apart from initially announcing the news to her I cannot speak any more about beautiful little Daisy Margaret Tyler. I am glad to be well enough to visit Isabel on the ward; it so happened that I was having one of my dialysis sessions when Donald appeared with the glad tidings after receiving the phone call at home that we had all been waiting for. Poor Isabel endured the birth alone, but as far as I can tell both mother and baby are doing well.

It's a long walk from the dialysis unit to the maternity ward, and so Donald pushes me in a wheelchair. I feel old, worn out and useless, but I am only 48 years old. Whatever is happening to my body?

Isabel cries when she sees me; whether it's the pregnancy hormones or the fact that I probably look so terrible I'm not sure, but to see her in tears causes a similar eruption in myself, especially when I catch sight of the baby. Ross, totally unaware of what his wife has been through, struts over like a proud father to envelop me in a hug, gives a pleasant greeting to Donald, and then picks up Daisy and puts her into my arms. I hear Donald giving a curt acknowledgment back to Ross, but all my senses are focused on my little granddaughter; the fine blonde, downy hair, the little button nose, and the heart-shaped face just like Isabel's. I hold her close to me as she sleeps the slumber of the innocent.

All around me are happy, healthy mothers and new-born babies. I wonder where the time has gone; it seems like only yesterday I held Isabel in my arms, pleased and proud of myself for bringing her into the world. I have no idea if I will live to see little Daisy grow up. The Lord giveth, and the Lord taketh away. I think He plays games with us, rolling the dice to see whose turn it will be to die tomorrow. If the dice show a 4 and an 8, then somebody aged 48 gets a turn at passing through the pearly gates……

Isabel brings me out of my reverie as she wipes her eyes and grins.

"What do you think of her, Mum?"

I sigh; there are few words to describe the feeling of holding your first grandchild.

"She's adorable." I feel tears behind my eyes struggling to get out. "Treasure every moment with her; she will be grown before you know it."

Out of the corner of my eye I see Isabel sit up straighter in the bed, and then reach out to touch her daughter's fingers.

"I'm going with Ross when the band start their tour at the end of September. I'll be breastfeeding but Daisy will be no trouble; she'll still be at that very portable stage. Ross wants us with him, Mum. Sorry, but if the band are playing locally I'll pop in and see you. This tour will be a great chance for them to get noticed by all the right people."

"You go where your husband is, darling." I try and hide my disappointment. "But how will you cope on the road? How do you wash for instance?"

Isabel laughs and looks at Ross, who grins at me while avoiding Donald's gaze.

"All the venues have showers, Marian. I'm a very clean boy."

"We'll cope, Mum; don't worry." Isabel gives my arm a squeeze. "You just concentrate on getting well again."

"I do feel a bit better on the dialysis." I nod at Isabel. "It's just a question of waiting for a transplant."

I am aware of Donald standing stiffly like a statue behind me. I turn around in the chair and pass Daisy to him:

"Here; have a hold of your granddaughter. Isn't she lovely?"

I see his face soften for a moment as he looks down on the baby and then up again at Isabel. I notice that Daisy has a similar hair colouring to Ross, but I hear Donald making no reference to the fact.

"She looks like *you*, Izzy."

"Ross's parents said the same." Isabel nods at her father. "Perhaps the next one will favour Ross."

Donald grunts and resumes his statue-like position at the bedside. I feel sorry for Ross; he's excited about the birth of his daughter and is trying to be pleasant, but as far as I can tell is receiving no comeback at all from his new father-in-law. Isabel and myself ignore the atmosphere between the two men, and chatter on regardless as we've always done. My daughter, in my opinion, is slightly tearful and obviously missing her sister. She whispers to me as she reaches over and takes the baby back from my aching arms.

"Do you think Clare will come and see the baby, Mum?" I hate to disappoint her, but I shake my head. "Sorry, but maybe when more time has gone past." "Tell her she's always welcome." "I will."

I think it only right to leave Isabel and Ross with their baby for the remaining visiting time, and we say our goodbyes. As Donald manoeuvres the wheelchair away from the bed I look back and see them together, obviously happy in each other's company and enthralled with the new life they have created. My face shows abject disapproval as I sigh and look up at Donald, now pushing me furiously along the corridor.

"You could have been more pleasant to Ross. He's your son-in-law now."

"Bloody good-for-nothing long haired dropout if you ask me."

The wheelchair is going so fast that I fear I may be propelled into orbit. I shake my head at him.

"He's working hard and earning money for his family by doing what he's good at; singing and playing guitar. You work at what you're good at; we can't all be blessed with the same talents."

"Waste of space; look how he's turned the girls against each other. Izzy's given up a good career. It's a bloody nightmare."

My husband seems adamant in his hatred for Ross. Our family is broken; split down the middle. I fail to see how the rift will ever be healed.

CHAPTER 17

CLARE

SO, THE BABY is born, blatant evidence of their intimacy. My stomach twists in knots imagining them together, consummating their marriage or cooing over their new-born, which Mum says looks the image of Izzy. I don't want to see Izzy, Ross or the baby. Apparently I hear from Mum that my sister wants me to visit, but I've told Mum I'd rather stab myself in the eye with a red hot poker. She's gone off with him on tour now, so at least I can go home and not worry that she'll be there.

I'm really enjoying the second year English course at Uni. Next year we'll start the teacher training as well. It's all riding on me to do well as Izzy is now the boring *hausfrau*. Let her get on with it is what I say; she made her bed and now she has to lie in it. If only Ross wasn't lying in it too, but I know I have to move on and forget him.

At long last I've managed to ditch Tony, after weeks of putting up with him following me around the campus like some lovesick puppy. Ruth's boyfriend Tim suggested a foursome with his friend James McVie recently, and even from our first date James and I are getting on really well. We even had sex on our second date. I can't believe how stupid and naïve I was to faff about so indecisively about whether or not I should lose my virginity to Ross. If only I could have that time back again; Ross would never have passed me over for Izzy a second time, of that you can be assured. All I have to do is remember to take my little white pill every morning. It's amazing; such sexual freedom we young women have nowadays compared to our mothers and grandmothers. I thank the good lord every day that I am growing up in the 1970's.

I'm worried about Mum. If she's not asleep she's shuffling around the house like an old woman, trying to do the things she used to do. I thought people with kidney disease got better with dialysis? I have a niggly feeling that she's not keeping to the strict diet or restraining her liquid intake. Her legs are very swollen. I try and help her as much as I can when I'm not at Uni or out with James, but I can see her old sparkle has gone and she's only a shell of the person she was before. It's terrible that neither me, Izzy or Dad are suitable donors for her. Poor Mum has nobody; we're her only true family.

I should be at home looking after Mum, but James wants me to stay and hear the band later on in the student bar. It's her dialysis treatment today, and I know Dad will pick her up after his clinic finishes. I try and phone to let her know I'll be late, but all I get is Dad's new answering machine. I leave a message before grabbing something to eat in the food hall, and then walk back to the digs that James lives in with four other guys from his year. At 21 and an Applied Maths student, he's older than the rest as he had a gap year where he went off to do something wonderful with deprived kids in Africa. On his bedroom wall he has photos of the poor children he helped. Five little street urchins. They seem inordinately happy though, and look out at me with shining eyes and pearly white teeth.

James is a good diversion from Ross. I love his shoulder-length dark blond hair. We have time to make slow, delicious love before the others come back to the flat. He is considerate enough to ensure that not just his own needs are met. When we are spent I lay myself down on top of him and listen to his heart gradually returning to its normal slower rhythm, while his fingers trace a line up and down my backbone, making me shiver.

"I'm glad you dumped that wanker." James intertwines his legs with mine and folds his arms around me. "I don't know what you saw in him.

"Neither do I." I realise now that I was on the rebound from Ross. "He kept going on about getting married."

"Jesus Christ; you had a lucky escape."

We can hear the others returning. We lock ourselves in the bathroom together and have a quick shower, giggling at the incessant tapping and shouting of what I presume is sexual innuendo in Latin through the frosted glass pane from Alan Lord, a second year Classics man, eager to use the toilet. James opens his mouth and yells '*Age quod agis!*' We wrap ourselves in towels, unlock the door, and laugh as we run past Alan up the passageway and back to the privacy of the bedroom to get dressed again in peace.

"What did you say to him?" I yank the towel away from his lower half and enjoy the sight of his naked body.

"Oh, I told him to go off and do his thing somewhere."

James kisses me and the temptation to carry on where we left off is overwhelming, but with Alan and the others about it's not a good time. We slope off back to the student bar, have a few beers, and listen to the band. They're more folky than rock, and not to our taste. I look at my watch; it's quarter past ten and I've got a whole day of Chaucer tomorrow.

"I must go home." I give James a kiss.

"I'll run you home in the car."

James has the good fortune to have received a second hand car from his parents for his 21st birthday, a well preserved Ford Escort in a vivid shade of yellow. I call it Kiki, as it has the number plate KKE 519H. We clamber in for the short journey back home. As we turn the corner into my road I assume my parents are already in bed, as there are no lights left on.

"That's strange." I look at James as he brings Kiki to a halt. "They don't usually go to bed until I'm home."

"I'll come in with you if you like?"

James turns off the engine and I climb out of the passenger seat. I open the front door, switch on the hall light, and go into the front room. My mother is laying on the settee and I scream, because even to my untrained eye she looks very, very dead.

CHAPTER 18

DONALD

IF ONLY SOFIA hadn't gone off sick. If only somebody else had been there to take the emergency bullous pemphigoid admission. If only Marian had phoned for a taxi to take her to dialysis instead of swallowing all those sleeping pills she might still be here, but as I look out the window and see even more floral tributes arriving in the garden I realise that probably dialysis wouldn't have saved her in the long run anyway. She took no regard of either mine or the dietitian's advice; it's as though she wanted to die. The depression she was probably born with had been rife these past few years. She was adopted, but had never suffered anguish through wanting to find her birth mother, so God knows why she was never happy; we had enough money and a good lifestyle. I kept the affairs from her; she never knew what went on outside her own little world. Women are a conundrum to me, and always will be.

Isabel is staying away from the house and will meet us at

the crematorium. I miss her upbeat slant on life; so different from her mother's. Hopefully the boy is still on tour; all I want to do when I see him is forget the Hippocratic Oath and punch his lights out. I expect the baby will scream throughout the service, as babies do.

I try to comfort Clare, but nothing I do or say seems to make any difference; the girl needs her mother. It would be preferable if my daughters were on speaking terms, but Clare's hatred of her sister still runs deep and is unrelenting.

I can see the undertakers outside with the hearse. I notice that my wreath has been given pride of place next to the coffin. Clare sits weeping on the settee with the new boyfriend. It seems I am redundant now as far as providing any sort of emotional crutch for my daughter; all she needs from me is the money in my bank account. I was never brought up to be demonstrative, but the sight of the boyfriend holding Clare in his arms brings a rampant jealousy surging to the fore; not the sort of emotion needed on the day of your wife's funeral.

I do not know who half the people are that are in my house. When they have all dispersed to their cars I fasten a black tie, lock the front door, and follow Clare and James into the waiting hearse. I feel sad that Isabel is not by my side at this occasion. She knows to seat herself well away from Clare at the crematorium, which will no doubt be somewhere at the back. I was hoping the funeral might have brought them together, but it has, in fact, had quite the opposite effect.

We travel in silence to the crematorium. I hope the vicar still has the little eulogy I prepared. I think Marian would have wanted a religious ceremony; all our married life I tried to give her what she wanted, and her funeral today is no exception. It's not possible for a man to stay faithful to one woman for his entire life, but my wife wanted for nothing. We enjoyed an upper middle-class lifestyle; both girls loved their private schools, and there is nothing in the world that I would not have done for any of them.

A man needs a little pleasure; it means nothing and indeed it *is* nothing. Marian needed never to worry on that account, but somehow, thinking about it, I wonder if she suspected anything? We will never know. She takes that knowledge with her to the grave.

Isabel is waiting outside the entrance to the crematorium alongside Marian's friends from the hospital. The baby seems to be asleep in its pushchair. I give Isabel a hug as I step outside the hearse and take a quick look at my granddaughter before going into the small chapel; thankfully the infant doesn't resemble its father. Clare and James go straight in without even acknowledging Isabel, and I take a seat next to Clare in the front row. I've no idea where Isabel is sitting, and I don't want to turn around and be the recipient of all those pitying stares.

The vicar gives a short, sweet service. Everybody pretends to sing the hymns, as is normal on occasions such as these. All I can hear is the organ blasting away and the vicar's booming bass rising above it. I cannot feel much emotion at all. I try to imagine Marian lying there in her coffin on the bier, but the whole scenario feels as though it's happening to somebody else.

My granddaughter wakes up and begins to be rather vociferous. I hear footsteps in the aisle, and realise that Isabel must have taken the baby outside. I would give away all the money in my bank account to the no-good son-in-law if I could follow her out at this precise moment. However, no; I must watch the coffin move noiselessly on well-oiled rollers through the curtains, as they close on a life that should have been mine for at least another thirty years or more.

It is in the evening when the finality of the situation hits home. Clare has gone off somewhere with James, and I am in the house alone. I must get used to cooking for myself and even worse, washing up afterwards. I am not cut out for this kind of domesticity. Marian always ran the house with her usual effortless aplomb, and I do not have the time to take over her household duties. My daughter is more often away than at home, and to be fair at her age she should not be expected to take over where her mother left off. I will need to employ some kind of housekeeper. Is there still such a thing these days?

Did I love my wife? Yes, I am sure that undoubtedly I did. However, I am perturbed that I still feel no great emotion at the fact that she is dead. Why is this so? Did we become so estranged from each other over the years that we were eventually leading separate lives? Did she love *me*? I assume so, but will never know for sure.

I sit in Marian's chair at the dining table, thinking of all the meals she prepared that I never ate, and of her waiting up faithfully all those nights for me to come home from some woman's bed. I realise that on the whole, I must have been a bit of a bastard. This makes me no better than the loathsome son-in-law.

I sit staring into space until the tears begin to fall.

CHAPTER 19

CLARE

DAD SEEMS A changed man. I didn't think that Mum's death would affect him so badly. He's not bothering to cook for himself unless I'm home to do it, and even if I serve up something he likes he's pushing most of the food around the plate. If he's not working then he sits around in his dressing gown staring at the TV.

I'm starting to feel responsible for his welfare. I miss Mum like crazy. James drives me home after Uni every night now, and I cook for the three of us. Dad seems to like James, who has the knack of bringing Dad out of his shell when he's here. It's got to the point where I'm thinking of asking Dad if James can move into Izzy's old room. Of course I can't let on to Dad that we sleep together and we'd have to be a bit discreet about it, but at least James' parents wouldn't need to pay all that rent for his digs, and we'd have a bit more privacy.

As James holds his breath I decide to bring the subject up at dinner.

"Do you like the pie, Dad?"

"Very nice."

Dad is a man of few words. As he eats I gauge his mood, which seems unusually good-tempered this evening.

"Can I ask you something?"

"What?"

Dad, about to bring a forkful of steak pie to his lips, looks up at me quizzically as I pop the dreaded question.

"What do you think about James moving into Izzy's old room?"

"What do I think?"

"Yes." I glance at James, who is hanging on Dad's every word.

"What's wrong with where he is now?"

James interrupts me just as I begin to reply.

"Well, Doctor Ronson, I'm less than happy sharing with several noisy students who are mainly nocturnal, and plus the fact I love Clare and want to be with her as much as I can. My parents would obviously pay for my food and keep."

The silence is deafening. I look at Dad, waiting for a change of expression or some sign that he is going to agree. Dad looks at James, chews his steak in a thoughtful manner, and then quite nonchalantly gives us his answer.

"James, if we're going to meet on the upstairs landing in the mornings, then I expect you'd better call me Donald."

I hear Dad leaving a message on Izzy's answerphone to ask her to take home anything she wants out of her old room, all of which he is going to put in the loft for storage. I know she's on tour with Ross, so I have no idea when she'll come back home. My guts get all twisted up when I think of what I've missed out on, and so I try not to let the thought of them cloud my days and weeks. I can't help following the band's progress in *Melody Maker* though. It seems that 'Kick' are making a name for themselves in the world of rock. As we move into November I scan down the article for their next gig; they're obviously filling larger venues now with their new manager, and will next play at the Hammersmith Odeon on Saturday November 13th. There's a picture of Ross and Darryl on Stage at The Lyceum; I cut it out with the article, and add it to the scrapbook I started last month. Both Ross and his brother now have hair reaching down to their mid-back; they look absolutely gorgeous, and I suddenly want to cry again for all I've lost through my own stupidity.

James has moved in. As far as Dad is concerned we're just good friends. Thank goodness they've both taken a liking to each other, and there's none of those awkward silences that we have any time that Dad sees Ross. I feel like showing Dad my scrapbook and letting him know that Ross is probably earning quite a lot of money now, but at the last minute think better of it.

With my new burgeoning relationship with James and keeping up with my studies, my life is pleasantly full, but nothing can take the place of Mum. Living in a house of non-talkative men I miss the girly chats I used to enjoy with Mum. I would come home from school or Uni, and there she'd be if she'd worked an early shift, eager to find out about my day. Most of the time Dad is working at the hospital, and it's James and I who come home first and prepare the evening meal. Dad had Mum running around after him for so many years that he seems incapable of looking after himself. I'm sure he thinks the dirty laundry cleans itself and that the carpet gets vacuumed by elves overnight. But I mustn't complain; he's very generous with money, and to some extent I suppose I'm spoiled in that regard, however, I'd live on a pittance if I could have Mum back again.

I check my savings account at the Post Office, and am surprised to find out that I have nearly £350. That evening while Dad is out on call, James and I take advantage of his absence and make rather frantic love for what seems a very long time. As we cuddle up afterwards, I lay on my back with my head on his shoulder, and hope I've picked the right moment.

"James….."

"What?" He twists a lock of my hair around his finger and kisses the top of my head. "Whatever it is, the answer's *yes.*'

"I was just about to ask if you fancied going to a concert on Saturday night. I'm paying, by the way."

"How can I refuse an offer like that?" He chuckles and wraps his arms around me.

"Apparently 'Kick' are playing at the Hammersmith Odeon. We can go up on the train; maybe stay in a hostel overnight? What do you say?"

"Kick?" He yawns. "Never heard of them."

"I have; they're very good."

"Whatever; yeah, go for it. As long as you're paying then!"

"Done; I'll phone the box office tomorrow and order some tickets."

I can't help but have a smile on my face as I lay there next to him. At long last I'm going to see Ross again on Saturday night. I wonder about trying to get into the band's dressing room, but then realise that Izzy will probably be sitting there waiting for him. I turn back to James, kiss him, and bury my face in his chest.

CHAPTER 20

ROSS

GOD, THE LUXURY of not having to haul all the equipment out of the trailer, up the ramp, into the venue, and then do the reverse of the whole bloody thing all over again after the gig. There's no glamour in being dog tired and sweaty at two o'clock in the morning, knowing you've got another hour of backbreaking work ahead of you before you can climb into your bunk on the tour bus. It certainly helps being able to afford roadies this time. Only a year ago we were unknowns playing the Portsmouth pub circuit. Now thanks to Parlaphone's A&R scout we now have a hefty advance to make a new album, and we're now playing awesome venues like The Lyceum and the Hammersmith Odeon. Sometimes I wonder if I'm going to wake up and find out it's all been a dream.

Izzy and Daisy, bless them, have taken to the road like ducks to water. Izzy at the end of the day is just one of the lads, and fortunately Daisy is a contented baby who at the moment just sleeps and feeds all the time. I know everything will change as she becomes older and we'll either have to find a nanny for her for the next tour, or she'll stay at home with Izzy. However, we're enjoying being new parents at the moment, even though we're bunking in the tour bus with 14 other guys.

My love for Izzy surprises even me sometimes; I want her with me day and night. I bless the day I found Clare wandering around on Desolation Hill. If I hadn't met Clare I would never have known Izzy. I feel a complete prick that Clare was so devastated when I took up with her sister, but it's like Izzy and I were made for each other. Clare is a lovely girl, who at the time was just not ready for a proper relationship. I hear now that there's a new boyfriend moved into Izzy's old room, and I'm happy for Clare; she deserves to be loved, but just not by me.

I can't sleep; we didn't get off stage at the Glasgow Apollo until 11.30pm, and the adrenaline is still pumping even though it's 4am. Sometimes the swaying of the bus, a few downers or a joint can lull me asleep, but not tonight; we're on our way to London to play at the Hammersmith Odeon later this evening. Our support guys will go on first, but I know they're as nervous as we are. All the excitement goes to Chaz's stomach, and he often has to climb out of the bus to throw up.

I'm sitting on my bunk watching Izzy feed Daisy opposite. There's such a serene expression on my wife's face; it's awesome watching the two of them. Daisy loves the motion of the bus; the guys tell me they never hear her cry at all. Izzy is smiling at me and all I want to do is lay on top of her, but *that* will definitely have to wait.

We're pulling into a service station; probably Chaz has the squits again. Archie the driver is adamant that none of us are allowed to shit in the chemical toilet downstairs. I bet *he* does. With 16 of us living on uppers, our nerves and surviving on crap food, it's a wonder more of us haven't come down with Rameses' Revenge. Izzy will get out and use the loo whether she wants to go or not. I can't make out why women do that; why go through the bother of getting out of bed and walking through the car park to the toilets when you don't need to go? Still, it'll give me a chance to cuddle my daughter and marvel at her little features that are so like Izzy's, although I think she has quite a different personality; more laid back like me.

When Izzy comes back she gives me a kiss and then takes Daisy and puts her in her Moses basket at the end of her bunk. I pull the curtains across and lay back on the pillow, willing sleep to claim me for a few hours.

I must have dozed off eventually, because when I wake up the bus has come to a halt at one of the London service stations, ready for us to have a shower and breakfast. I can hear the other guys waking up. I feel sorry for Izzy having to put up with the guys farting 24/7, but she seems cool with it; she's even nicknamed the bus *The Fartorium*. The guys love her, but I can see they also have a great respect for her, and that's good.

Breakfast; something unhealthy that my mother would not want me to eat, I expect. I yawn and stretch, and feel excited about the day ahead. The curtains open and there is my wife's sleepy face looking in at me. She rubs her eyes and climbs into my bunk for a quick cuddle.

"Morning; you were snoring worse than Andy last night."

"I wasn't; it was probably Darryl next door." I grin and give her a kiss. "Daisy still asleep?"

"Yeah. I'm going to show her the sights of Hammersmith today while you're setting up."

"Good luck with that then." I chuckle and fold my arms around her. "Are there any sights in Hammersmith?"

"There's the Lyric theatre, I think. Perhaps I'll take her to see a play and introduce her to a bit of culture."

"Awesome."

My wife and daughter are armchair travellers, or rather *Fartorium* travellers; one day in Scotland, the next Ireland, Wales or England. Izzy takes Daisy out in the pushchair during the day wherever we happen to be, and rocks her to sleep in the dressing room at night to the sounds of *Kick*. Usually by the time all the gear is loaded back in the trailer and we're ready to go, they are both back on the bus and dead to the world. It's a strange kind of life for them, but at the moment they're both thriving on it. Long may it continue; at the moment I wouldn't want to go on the road without them.

CHAPTER 21

IZZY

THERE'S A SPECIAL thrill about being backstage. Daisy and I are thriving on the atmosphere. However, I also like to do a little bit of sightseeing wherever we happen to be, and so I decide that after I've fed Daisy I'm going to saunter out with the pushchair while the boys are sound-checking and see what I can see.

My daughter is a greedy little madam; the feed is finished in 15 minutes. I stand at the side of the stage and signal to Ross that I'm going out. So busy are the band and roadies with setting up that I don't think he even registers I'm there.

There's a weak sun setting over the infamous Hammersmith roundabout as I exit by the stage door. Daisy gurgles contentedly in her pushchair as I start to walk down to the busy main road. To my surprise there's already an orderly queue of fans snaking around the corner from the main doors, waiting to beat each other down to the front as soon as the doors open. I will have to pass them to get up to the high street, and some of them turn to look at me as I flash my lanyard and ID badge, sidle past the bouncer at the stage door, and trundle along pushing the pram. One particularly cretinous youth in his late teens, bored with standing in the queue, leers suggestively in my direction.

"Alright darlin'?"

"Fuck off and swivel on it."

I tuck the lanyard back into my coat and push the pram a bit faster. Weeks of living at close quarters with 15 other guys has given me a mouth like a sewer. The youth's equally moronic contemporaries hoot with laughter at my remark.

As I near the head of the queue I see a girl wearing a purple midi-length dress that seems an exact replica of one I remember seeing in Clare's wardrobe. She has a black bomber jacket over the top, and is standing next to a tall guy wearing jeans and a denim jacket, who is sporting fashionable shoulder-length light brownish hair. The guy has his arm around her and they both have their backs to me. The girl's hair is slightly longer than Clare's, but she reminds me of my sister. I take a quick glance as I pass them, and freeze in shock. Clare stares back at me impassively; hatred oozing from every pore although her expression remains inscrutable.

I wrestle with my thoughts and try to decide if I should say anything or continue walking on. Eventually after what seems like an eternity but is probably only a few seconds, I smile and offer the olive branch.

"Hi."

I turn the pushchair around so that Clare can see Daisy. My sister ignores her niece completely, and turns back to her boyfriend without saying a word. Stunned, distraught, lost for words and conscious that I'm providing free entertainment for all Kick's waiting fans, I manoeuvre the pram past the rest of the queue and head towards the nearest zebra crossing, wishing to be anywhere except the place where I am at this particular moment.

It's a Saturday evening and the traffic is heavy. On the other side of the road I can see a tube station and a long parade of shops thronging with people. Shaking, I cross over and find a coffee house. I sink down into one of the plush chairs, rock the pram with one hand, and order a strong espresso when the waitress arrives. The urge to sightsee has completely gone, and all I want to do is run back to Archie and the safe haven of the tour bus parked in Queen Caroline Street. I bide my time. I will have to wait until the queue goes down and Clare goes inside the venue. I do not want to risk running into her again.

I am on my third coffee by the time the queue starts to move. Pretty soon as I glance through the traffic I can see only ticket touts and t-shirt sellers gathering up their wares outside the Odeon. I am buzzing with caffeine, Daisy is becoming restless, and it is time to head back.

The curtains have been pulled around the downstairs bus windows. Archie is obviously asleep and takes ages to unlock the door, his expression registering intense irritation at being woken up. I apologise, and escape upstairs to my bunk where Daisy falls fast asleep, leaving me to wonder what on earth I'm going to do with myself for the next four or five hours.

After reading until my eyes ache I eventually doze off but wake much later to the sound of the engine starting up; we are on the move again. I pull the cord to switch on the tiny wall light, and check my watch; the time reads twenty past two. Elsewhere in the bus I can hear the guys settling down for the night and Daisy stirring in her Moses basket. My breasts begin their familiar tingle as I hear her cry for a feed.

I sit up, reach over to the basket, scoop up my daughter and put her to the breast, pleased to see Ross's face peer around the curtain.

"Hey; I thought I heard her." He whispers. "I can't sleep; can I climb in?"

Nodding, I smile at him and shift over towards the wall.

"Don't be silly; you don't even have to ask. How did it go tonight?"

"Awesome!" He whispers. "You should have been there. We rocked the place!"

"I saw Clare in the queue with her boyfriend when I took the baby out for a walk." I hold Daisy closer. "Did she try and meet up with you afterwards?"

Ross props himself up on my pillows and stretches out on the bed. His hair is damp and there is a pleasant aroma of cannabis and soap. He yawns and shakes his head.

"No, but the security staff would have kept people away from the backstage area anyway."

"She was there in the queue to get in; I saw her."

"Well, as I say, she would have had trouble getting past Larry. He's built like a brick shit-house."

I giggle with him at the mental image of the formidable Larry, and lean towards him whilst still feeding Daisy.

"Love you; I'm having such a great time." I look up and kiss him. "So proud of you."

"We're only just beginning." Ross puts his arm around me, sighs, and gives me a squeeze. "Next year I just *know* we're going to be tax exiles."

"Can we buy an island and get away from it all?" I savour the image of palm trees rustling on white sands."

Ross chuckles and gives another yawn.

"Maybe the Isle of Dogs for now, but tomorrow....who knows?"

Daisy nods off during her feed. I pop her back in the Moses basket and snuggle up next to Ross. We both sleep, comforted by the presence of each other, our baby, and the rocking motion of the bus as it drives the band ever onwards to untold fame and glory.

CHAPTER 22

CLARE

WITH POSSIBLY EIGHT thousand people in the audience or thereabouts, I never thought I'd actually come across Izzy walking past while I am standing in the queue to get into the Hammersmith Odeon. Judging by the way she comes up to me and smiles, she obviously wants to make amends for poaching my boyfriend and luring away the love of my life. However, I am having none of it.

James wonders who she is, and why I refuse to speak to her. I have to explain to him that the woman with the baby is my sister, and she is married to Kick's singer and guitarist, but that we have fallen out badly and do not speak anymore. I decide not to tell him the reason why. James mentions that Izzy appears as though she wants to make amends, but I tell him to leave well alone and change the subject.

I am so desperate to see Ross. Standing there in the queue I feel I can almost reach out and touch him. We run to the front of the stage as soon as the doors open, but others can run faster and we end up quite near the stage but not actually in the front row. I want Ross to see me, no *pray* that he will see me, but if he does he gives no indication. He looks like the rock god he has become as he struts his stuff about on the stage. His hair is longer and he is slightly thinner, but my God, he is so, so *hot*. The fans scream for more, and I can see that the band have it made and will probably soon be millionaires. I still find it hard to believe that Izzy has snatched this all away from me.

After the gig I lie to James and tell him that I want to make amends with Izzy. I seek out the scary-looking bouncer by the side of the stage and explain to him that I am Ross's sister-in-law and that I want to congratulate him. The bouncer seems as wide as he is tall, and all I receive is a *'fuck off'* for my troubles. I used to be Ross's *girlfriend*, but now he is unattainable; I might just as well try to reach for the moon.

We pass by the tour bus parked in Queen Caroline Street on our way to a hostel for the night. All the curtains are drawn; I have no idea if Ross is in there or not, but I know *she* is. I can see a light on upstairs through the curtains, and I imagine her singing to the baby while she waits for Ross to finish backstage. It is only when James puts his arm around me that I come back to earth with a bump and remember who I am with. I try not to let my disappointment show, but James is not Ross, nor will he ever be.

There are beds available in a hostel we have found a few streets away from the venue. James kisses me and then disappears into the men's section, and I breathe a sigh of relief; I can now lie in bed and think about Ross in peace, and what we could have had together. All around me girls snore and mumble in their sleep as I let bitter tears fell onto my pillow at the thought of never being able to meet up with Ross ever again unless I make my peace with Izzy. I know I will wait for hell to freeze over before *that* happens.

Youth hostels are cheap, but there's always some gritty job you get allocated before you can leave the next morning. James and I have the task of cleaning the kitchen. There are years of grime on the cooker and work surfaces, and I come to the conclusion that nobody has ever cleaned it at all since the place was opened. We wipe a cloth over the surfaces, grin at the warden, and leg it along Queen Caroline Street back to the tube station. The tour bus is gone; all that is left is the space where it had been parked. I still have a leaflet in my pocket detailing the band's gigs, and I give it a quick glance as we wait for the tube. It seems that Ross and Izzy are now on their way across the Irish Sea to Belfast.

By the time we get back to Waterloo it is past lunch time. We grab a coffee and a sandwich at the station, and catch the 14.57 train to Portsmouth. I sleep for most of the way back on James' shoulder.

Kiki is still parked at Portsmouth station where we had left it. When we get home Dad is sitting at the dining table with a young-looking thirty-something woman I have never seen before. They are having dinner and chatting away as if they had known each other for years. I look over at the woman, who smiles at me.

"Hello. You must be Clare. I'm Rachel, a friend of your father's."

"Hello." I keep a cool tone to my voice as I answer the woman sitting so comfortably at my mother's table. "Yes I'm Clare; this is my boyfriend James."

"Hi." James reaches over to shake Rachel's hand. "Nice to meet you."

"Have you had dinner?" Dad looks up at me. "There's some salmon left."

"No thanks; we've eaten." I shake my head. "We'll go upstairs now."

When we reach the privacy of my room James looks at me in surprise.

"We haven't had any dinner; I'm starving! Why did you say that we'd already eaten?"

I brush off his remarks and with a wave of my hand.

"We can go out to the chip shop. Mum will be writhing in her grave at the thought of Dad sitting at her table with another woman."

"Life has to go on." James shrugs. "You wouldn't want him to spend the rest of his life on his own, would you?"

"Well, no…. but he could have waited a bit longer. The way they were so cosy together it makes me wonder if they've known each other a long time."

"It's not our business. Come on; let's go and get some fish and chips."

As we pass Dad's bedroom on our way downstairs again, the door is slightly ajar. I peep in and can see an unmade bed and some of Rachel's clothes strewn about on the floor. My heart sinks and I follow James down to the front door, eager to be gone from the knowledge that my father has found himself a young, attractive lover.

CHAPTER 23

DONALD

I CAN SEE Rachel's amused look as the front door slams.

"I don't think your daughter likes me very much."

I am sure Rachel is correct, but I tactfully try to find some words to soothe her ruffled feathers.

"Don't worry; she'll come around."

Rachel reaches for my hand across the table.

"I don't want to be the cause of bad feelings between you and your daughter. If you like I'll keep a low profile and stay away from the house."

I shake my head; the memory of Rachel and me laughing, naked and tangled up in the sheets last night is still fresh in my mind.

"If anything I want you here more, not less. We've known each other for so long. Now that your divorce from Lance is finalised, you're a free woman. Clare needs to realise that we're a couple now.

"I think she's worked that one out already."

I love it when Rachel laughs; that low, sexy laugh that is

filled with untold promise. Her burnished brown bob shimmers and shines in the lamplight. She twists her leg around mine under the table.

"So, I get rid of one man and hey presto, another one pops up?"

"Too right." I run a finger gently up and down her arm. "But just this one."

Rachel is good for me. She kept me sane through all the years of Marian's depression. I want her again badly, but have no idea when Clare and James will be back.

"How about I drive you home for cocoa? I'll leave a note for Clare. If we stay here we'll just have to hold hands all night."

"Now I know why I never had kids."

Clare will complain about the unwashed dishes, but I'll take a chance on that. I stand up and pull Rachel towards me.

"Do you know, you are the sexiest gynaecologist there ever was."

Rachel rubs herself against me.

"I'll take your word for it. Do you know many then?"

"No; just you and Ethan Lewis, but he does nothing for me."

"I quite like him." Rachel grins up at me. "I bet he could find my G-spot before you can say *atrophic vaginitis*."

"Oh God, I hope not; to both counts."

The radio plays a song I haven't heard for years; Joan Armatrading's *Willow*. We sway around the kitchen and I hold Rachel close. I feel happier than I have in years.

"I want to be *your* fireside." I kiss her neck.

"More like get me down on a fur rug by the fireside."

Rachel nibbles my ear.

"So what are we waiting for?"

Rachel has one of those homes in which every item of oak furniture has its undisturbed place and is bees-waxed to within an inch of its life. The cushions are always plumped up, and no dirty laundry is ever glimpsed by the naked eye. It is a house that has never seen a child's grubby hands, but right now the latter statement is exactly the reason I have driven here.

Our clothes are off before we even reach the bedroom. It is a crying shame to disturb the pressed and pristine brilliantly white percale duvet, but needs must. Her body has never failed to excite me beyond measure, and tonight is no exception. I savour every inch of her; the taut breasts unblemished from breastfeeding, the flat abdomen bearing no trace of any stretch marks, and the long slender legs, now parted for my pleasure. A wonderful testament to healthy eating and hours in the gym. She is a veritable goddess. Marian was once like Rachel as I remember, but that was many moons and two children ago.

She moans softly as I enter her, and for a few exquisite moments we are both lost in each other. I can imagine no greater joy at this precise moment.

"Mmmmm......"

She arches her back, but I come too quickly. She always has that effect on me.

"Don't stop......."

With my own needs satisfied I can watch the beauty of her face while her body reaches its climax. When at length her limbs lose their tension I ease myself down on top of her, letting my arms take some of my weight and rubbing my nose against hers.

"I like being your fireside."

She chuckles and wraps her legs around me.

"You're very good at it; I'm definitely alight, that's for sure."

I'm singing to a Joan Armatrading CD I found in the car as I drive home. It must have been one of Marian's; I don't remember ever purchasing it. I know I'm tone deaf, and must only sing when I'm alone, but tonight the lyrics of *Willow* hold an extra significance. I know Rachel is enjoying living on her own, but the male instinct to provide and protect is uncommonly strong in me, and I start to wonder how to bring the subject around to cohabiting. I will also need to try and bring Clare round to the idea of Rachel possibly moving in. The thought of my mistress of twelve years sharing my bed on a permanent basis brings a smile to my face as I reach home and park the car in the driveway.

It's late. The house is in darkness as I turn the key in the lock. As I fumble for the light switch I hear the unmistakeable sounds of sex coming from the direction of Clare's bedroom. I'm an expert at it by now. I turn on the light in the passageway and creep upstairs; the noises cease, and all that can be heard is the Grandfather clock ticking away on the landing.

As I close my bedroom door I realise that I can no longer dictate to my daughter. She is a grown woman, and to prevent her from having sex would be like trying to hold back the waves. I undress and fall into bed. The scent of Rachel is on my pillow, and it is somehow comforting in the loneliness of the night.

CHAPTER 24

RACHEL

DONALD WANTS TO meet up again tonight after my vulval clinic. I just *know* what he's building up to. However, after the farce of my marriage to Lance I'm now enjoying being an independent woman. Donald is a welcome distraction, but the last thing I want to do is intrude on his family life with his daughter. Clare would only resent me, as poor Marian is hardly cold in her grave.

Although I am pushing 40 this is the first time I have lived on my own, and I'm actually enjoying the experience. I can have the house just as I like it, and have complete control over which TV channel I watch. Lance would always sulk if he had to watch one of my documentaries, and I would usually end up giving in to him. Also I have first-hand knowledge of what's coming in the future, through the tearful fifty-something women arriving at my vulval clinic. Donald will soon tire of me once I begin to suffer from the inevitable ovarian failure, and so I will need to hold on to my house and independence for as long as I can.

I question the ability of any person to stay faithful to one partner for his or her entire life. I know I am not capable of it, and neither are Donald or Lance. This rose-tinted idea of marriage is very overrated; I suspect it was initially invented to give women unable to work through childcare duties some sort of financial, but not necessarily emotional, stability. The men will do as they please anyway, but if these impecunious females have managed to persuade a man to tie the knot, then at least they might have some chance of getting him to pay for any children he begets. If it was up to me I would tie another one; not a marriage knot, but quite a tight one in the region of the vas deferens.

Sex is good; if only it did not produce children. Women need to be able to enjoy sex without suffering the side-effects of the birth control pill or worrying about a possible unwanted pregnancy. I have many anxieties regarding the pill, and it will take at least another generation or two to see if I am proved correct. No good can come of going against nature and flooding the female body with excessive doses of oestrogen, making it a sitting duck for thromboses or even breast, ovary and uterine carcinomas. If only women could turn their fertility on and off without chemical intervention, but I daresay this will not be feasible in my lifetime.

As soon as the last patient leaves and I have finished dictating to Caroline, Donald comes into the consulting room. My secretary picks up on the tense atmosphere and makes a hurried exit.

"You might have waited, Donald. Secretaries talk, you know." I look at him as I wash my hands.

"Let them. If they're not talking about us it'll be about somebody else."

"Yes, exactly; I'd rather it *was* about somebody else." He shrugs off my remark.

"Dinner tonight? Seven o'clock? Do you fancy Chinese? We could go to the Yellow Orchid."

He looks at me hopefully, and I know I'll have to get the conversation over with sooner or later. I decide to opt for sooner.

"Seven thirty. I have a lecture to prepare for my students."

"I'll book a table."

The last time I was at this restaurant was with Lance when I told him I wanted a divorce. I hold out the faint hope that we will not be shown to the exact same table, and my wish is granted. The restaurant is not too busy, and there is a cosy nook in one corner where we can talk undisturbed. We order a sharing platter for two, and while we wait for the food to arrive Donald fiddles with a set of chopsticks.

"I had an alternative reason for asking you to dinner tonight."

I am well aware of the reason, but feign ignorance and take a sip from my glass of wine.

"What's that?"

"To find out your reaction regarding putting our relationship on a more permanent footing."

His eyes are pleading. I keep my voice light and take another sip of wine.

"Is this a proposal?" I smile at him. "Another husband so soon after my divorce would be a terrible mistake, Don.

Really, I'm happy as we are."

"Actually, no. It wasn't a proposal of marriage; rather a proposal of co-habitation."

"I see."

I am momentarily saved by the waiter bringing a sizzling array of fare. As I begin to eat I realise that Donald is still staring at me, waiting for a reply.

"Let's just be happy together just as we are. It's worked for us all these years." I stare down at my spring roll.

"I want you with me."

He sounds like a spoilt child who cannot get his own way. I hide a sigh of frustration and stick to my guns.

"Your daughter would resent me in the house; her mother has not long passed away. Leave it at least another year and then ask me again."

"You can be bloody sure I'm going to do just that."

His face is grim. I know only too well that in one year's time we will have to go through exactly the same charade, but then Marian's passing will not be considered a good enough excuse to reply again in the negative. At least I have another 12 months to come up with a suitable reason.

Donald is quiet as he drops me back home. I know another lovemaking session will put us both in a good mood, and so I invite him in for coffee. As usual, we never get around to actually drinking any.

CHAPTER 25

CLARE

MOST OF THE time now James and I have the house to ourselves. Dad is often at Rachel's house, and he usually stays over there at weekends. It seems strange to think of Dad having a sex life. I have a feeling he heard us making love when he crept up the stairs a few days ago. He never said anything, but he seems to accept it now when he sees James coming out of my room in the mornings. I suppose we'll both have to recognise each other's partners, but it seems so soon since Mum died.

Dad has mentioned inviting Rachel over for Christmas dinner. I know he wants me to like her, and so I'm going to have to make a superb effort in that direction. James thinks she's quite sexy, and so I can't get any sense out of him, but I worry that maybe she's trying to jump on a gravy train although Dad says she is a consultant at the hospital, like him. Perhaps she's just lonely.

What do I buy her for a Christmas present?   She always

looks so elegant, so I can't buy her a t-shirt from the market, which is more my style. James suggests perfume, but I have a feeling her taste is too expensive for my pocket. I think I'll browse around the bookshops and see what I can find in that direction.

This year is my first Christmas without Mum. She would always decorate the house and make it welcoming and homely, but I can't see how we're all going to enjoy ourselves; not only will Mum never celebrate another Christmas, but now I've also fallen out with Izzy there doesn't seem much to get excited about.

New Musical Express says that with a successful tour behind them, Kick are now one of the brightest upcoming stars of the rock world. Dad told me yesterday that Izzy and Ross visited him at Rachel's house with the baby, to let him know they're moving into a detached place with five bedrooms somewhere in South London. Dad lets on that he and Rachel have already had an invite to visit Izzy and Ross when they've moved in. Cosy. It sounds like they're in the money. I say to Dad that I don't really want to know what my sister and her husband are up to at all, and to not tell me anything more unless I ask. He agrees, with some reluctance. I cannot bear to think of them; rich, successful and in love. It's like someone is twisting a knife in my heart; it should have been *me*.

Dad must be getting senile; from what he says he seems to have accepted Ross at last. Perhaps it's because of all the money he's earned from the tour. Dad has always been rather avaricious in that respect, and what with the big London house as well I expect Dad is quite impressed, although thankfully he doesn't keep going on about it.

The dreaded day has arrived. I can hear Dad singing in the shower as he waits for Rachel to arrive. I got up especially early to stuff the turkey and put it in the oven, but feel like saying *stuff it* to Dad and disappearing with James over to visit his parents. However, I've got to bond with the woman who no doubt is already envisioning becoming my stepmother. When the doorbell rings Dad is shaving, James is still in his pyjama shorts upstairs, and so I have to face the *Rachel*.

"Hello Clare! Happy Christmas!"

Rachel swans into the house as though she owns it, carrying presents and wafting perfume behind her as she walks. I give her a smile which doesn't quite reach my eyes, matching her own false good humour.

"Happy Christmas. Dad's still getting ready."

"Oh, I'll soon sort *him* out."

To my surprise as I watch she runs upstairs, opens the bathroom door (she must know that we don't have a lock), stands in the doorway and starts chatting to Dad. I am astounded that she has the nerve to do this in our house, and I stand open-mouthed at the foot of the stairs until some of my anger dissipates. James appears on the upstairs landing half naked and still in his pyjama shorts, but Rachel is obviously unconcerned. I hear her laughing with James as I stomp off to the kitchen to check on the turkey and peel mounds of vegetables.

To my relief Rachel stays upstairs with Dad in his room. This gives me a chance to prepare the meal and set the table. James has a quick shower and comes downstairs.

"Where is she now?" I hiss at James as he enters the kitchen.

"They're still in Donald's room with the door closed." James keeps his voice low.

"How rude!" I bash a lid onto one of the saucepans of vegetables to make my point. "She just about managed to say *hello* before she disappeared."

"Probably wanted to keep out of your way." James shrugs. "You're hardly exuding good cheer and seasonal greetings."

"Don't *you* start!" I sigh with venom. "It's going to be like having the bloody Angel of Death sitting at the table."

"Come on, cheer up; it's Christmas." James comes over to give me a kiss. "Do you want to open your present now or later?"

"Later; let's get rid of those two first. We can escape upstairs after dinner. I'm cooking it, so I'm not washing up. Perhaps *she* can get her hands wet, seeing as she's made herself at home already."

"Another saucer of milk darling?"

James dodges a tea towel expertly, laughing as he picks it up off the floor. Then he puts it around my neck and pulls me towards him as I stand by the stove.

"My little domestic goddess. Give the lady a break; she's probably too nervous to come down."

"Bog off." I turn back to the cooker with the hint of a smile on my face.

"If you're not nice today, then you're not getting your present."

"I don't want one anyway."

"You will when you see it."

My curiosity is aroused, but first there is the ordeal of Christmas dinner to get through.

"Can I do anything to help?"

Rachel looks as disinterested as I usually am in anything remotely culinary. I shake my head.

"It's all done, but I'm not washing it all up though." I cannot help the last remark; it sort of slips out of its own accord.

"I'll get some wine from the cellar." Dad smooths over the awkward moment. "Have you seen our cellar, Rachel?"

I expect they've even had sex down there at some time or another, so at home she seems to be in our house. As Rachel follows Dad down to the basement I glare at her retreating back and roll my eyes at James.

"This is lovely, Clare. The turkey is cooked to perfection."

Rachel reaches over for some more cranberry sauce and shoots me a glance from under her shiny fringe.

"Mum always cooked it for five hours, and so that's what I did."

I see Rachel look uncomfortable at the mention of Mum. I give a hollow smile, while my thoughts stray elsewhere: *So she should flinch, the bitch. She and my father were probably screwing for years while my mother was still alive.*

"It's very tasty."

"Thank you."

An awkward silence follows, broken only by James as he undertakes his usual peacekeeping duties.

"Shall we pull the crackers?"

I nod in agreement and try to look as if I am enjoying myself as the crackers are opened. Rachel has obviously decided not to mess up her hair, and keeps her party hat on the table. I seize my chance.

"Party hats on! Come on, it's Christmas!"

I pull the stupid hat down over my ears, and spear a slice of turkey with my fork. Rachel perches her hat very carefully on her head, and Dad looks most uncomfortable in his attempts to emanate jovial Christmas cheer. Me, I stuff myself silly with as much food as my stomach can hold, and then James and I make a hasty exit, leaving *love's elderly dream* to argue over which one of them is going to do the washing up.

In the privacy of my room I open the present from James, while he fidgets impatiently about on the bed. It's a small box-shaped parcel, wrapped in pink tissue paper. I peel off several layers of tissue to reveal a smaller box, and take off the lid. Inside I can see a diamond ring; a solitary jewel glinting in the overhead light. I look up at James; my mouth making a small 'o' of surprise.

"Yes it is." He says, and nods. "So….will you?"

"Will I what?" I stall for time, not believing what is happening.

"Marry me when we finish Uni." He states.

I look at the ring, and then tenderly lift it out of the box. I see a way out from having to live with Dad and put up with the Angel of Death. I see a kind, generous man in front of me, and a good provider for my future babies.

"Of course I will." I kiss him. "This is the best Christmas present I've ever had!"

PART 2 – 4th JUNE 2002

CHAPTER 26

CLARE

THE IRONY OF the situation is not lost on me as I lie in bed waiting for Lauren to wend her way home from Newport. I had hoped she would avoid hearing about the festival's resurgence, but unfortunately I think our intrepid, independent and fearless daughter was one of the first in line for a ticket. Now I know just what my own mother went through whilst awaiting my safe return from Desolation Hill.

Beside me James sleeps the sleep of the righteous, even with knowing full well that Lauren and her friends will probably hitchhike the 200 miles home to Suffolk. I toss and turn under the duvet, imagining the perils that could befall three 20 year old girls who might have consumed too much alcohol. My suggestion of waiting at the ferry terminal with the car had been received with much derision and hoots of laughter. I am having a hard time facing the fact that my daughter is now a grown woman, and must live with the consequences of her actions.

It is 04:45 when I am awakened from a fitful sleep by a key turning in the lock downstairs. I leap out of bed like a startled fawn, rummaging around for my dressing gown and slippers. James snorts and turns over, but does not wake. I pad downstairs trying not to show how relieved I am that my daughter is still alive.

"Hi; good concert?"

Lauren bends down to let her rucksack slide off her back, and I shudder to think what could have happened on the road. Her legs in their terribly short shorts are long and brown and her blouse is tied under her bust, exposing a bare midriff, a rose tattoo, and a navel ring. I thank God that James is still asleep.

"Fantastic!" Lauren stands up and gives me a hug. "I'm going to have a shower now though, and then bed. See you later."

Although Lauren is home safely in the bosom of her family, thoughts of sleep are now driven from my mind. I cannot seem to settle, and decide to have some breakfast and wait for Matty's newspapers to be delivered. I will give him a bit of a head start and surprise him by having the papers all sorted when he surfaces around 6.30.

There is a thump of newspapers hitting the front doormat just as I hear Lauren stepping out of the shower and heading off towards her room. Papers on Tuesdays are easier to lift, lacking the weekend supplements that necessitate a vital halfway drop-off point to aid a 15 year old's under-developed musculature.

I have the bacon rolls ready and the addresses written on the corners of the front pages in what I think is the right order by the time I hear Matty's alarm sounding. Our morning routine is down to a fine art. Matty knows he only has two reminders to get his backside out of bed before I throw a hissy fit, and all the shouting usually wakes James anyway, who knows to physically lift Matty out of bed if he still has not risen by 06:45. Lauren is on a week's annual leave, and so I keep my voice down as I stomp upstairs, open Matty's bedroom door, and whisper fiercely.

"Your bacon rolls are getting cold, and the papers are ready to go."

The room is fusty and smells of teenage boy. I throw open the window and take a lungful of fresh air. A mumble comes from under the sheets.

"Thanks Mum."

I wonder yet again why Matty, never at his best first thing, volunteered so readily to do an early morning paper round. I know that if it wasn't for the fact that James teaches in the same school and therefore can drive him in, our son would miss the school bus with a depressing regularity.

The smell of frying bacon galvanises the boy into action. Matty appears at the kitchen door dressed in his school uniform at 06:40.

"I'm starving." He yawns. "Can I have two rolls?"

"A *please* would go down well." I slide a plate containing two bacon rolls towards him.

"*Please* can I *please* have the tomato sauce *please*?" Matty grins and bites into a roll.

"*Please* will you *please* hurry up and eat it *please*, you cheeky little bugger."

I grin back at him before going upstairs to get ready for work.

After years of stay-at-home childcare I was delighted to have been accepted as a teaching assistant at Lauren and Matty's old primary school. The extra money is a godsend, as one child is still at school and the other one earns only apprentice wages whilst studying to be a beautician and hairdresser. James has managed to climb the slippery slope to be head of the Mathematics department, but an actual headmastership and that oh-so-needed pay rise has so far eluded him.

I leave the house at 08:15, safe in the knowledge James will ensure Matty's timely arrival at school, and that my sleeping daughter needs no lift to the salon. The morning holds a promise of more heat to come, and experience tells me that all the children will be irritable and tired by two thirty this afternoon.

A blackbird scuttles past with a twig in its beak. I breathe in the still, warm air, pleasantly satisfied with my lot. We live in East Anglia, a beautiful part of the world, have two healthy children, and although we never had enough capital for a deposit on a mortgage, we can pay our bills and have enough money left over for a foreign holiday each year. It would have been nice if Lauren and Matty could have had their grandparents for a few more years, but it was not to be. Only Rachel survives, who often takes great delight in letting me know just what Izzy and Ross are getting up to. I am only too aware that time marches on, and people age and become infirm. However, I am still here, am grateful for my rude health, and even though I am 51 there is still no sign of the dreaded hot flushes. I am a lucky woman indeed. I sometimes wish I had not given up teaching so readily when the children came along, but James and I were both adamant at the time that we did not want anybody else bringing our children up. I sometimes look at my degree in its frame on the wall, and wonder if all the studying was worth it in the long run.

CHAPTER 27

ROSS

ALL FIVE GRANDCHILDREN rush to their favourite table, ready for their usual Saturday teatime treat. Le Belvedere never fails to impress with its spectacular views over the Dordogne River and lush, verdant fields on either side. My wife, somewhat tired with the heat I think, trails behind and chats to the staff in perfect French. I never did pick up the language very well, but Izzy, Daisy, Paul and the grandchildren are all bilingual. Izzy always did have a good brain in her head; at least she got to use it here by learning the local dialect. Me; all I can do is smoke a bit of weed, write a few songs, play some guitar and sing. I'm like a permanent foreigner in my own backyard.

We often visit Domme with the grandchildren; opposite Le Belvedere is the best ice cream parlour in the Dordogne, even catering for little Solenn's dairy intolerance. As if she knows what I am thinking, five year old Solenn looks at me with those limpid dark blue eyes so like her grandmother's.

"Maman dit que je dois seulement avoir la tarte de fromage de chevre."

Izzy arrives at the table and shakes her head.

"You need to speak English to Grandad; you know that."

I am saved from total embarrassment by my nine year old grandson Pierre.

"She has to eat the goat's cheese tart, Grandad." "Wonderful."

I smile at Solenn and give her a wink. She flashes a smile to melt my heart.

"Sorry, Grandad."

There is only a trace of a French accent. Paul's wife Laurence has been learning English alongside Solenn. She already speaks fluent German. I feel a total failure with my inability to grasp even basic French phrases. However, life is not too bad being a tax exile. I sit back in my chair, look down at the sun shining on the river, and realise that without the amount of money I have earned through being a part of 'Kick', none of my family would have been able to live the kind of lifestyle that they have become accustomed to over the years. I alone am responsible for all the family's continued wealth and happiness. My brother is useless with money; he spends it as soon as he earns it. Chaz blows it all on booze, but thankfully Andy's wife holds the purse strings, as does Izzy, who has made sure we invested wisely.

The waitress appears and Izzy rattles off everyone's orders. With her expertly coiffed hair, designer suit and sallow skin, she looks the epitome of a rich and elegant French socialite. She took to our new life here all those years ago like a duck to water. I think she is more at home in France now than she is in England.

The locals know who I am, but they don't bother me and treat me just as they would anybody else. We can go out as a family and remain unmolested, thank Christ. Going back to England is a different kettle of fish; fans are usually waiting for me at the airport. I have no idea how they find out I am travelling home, but they do. There must be somebody working at the airport who tips off the organisers of the fan club I expect. However, we can only go back to England for a few weeks every year now. Izzy is not too bothered about going back, due in part to the long rift still going on between her and her sister which Clare insists on perpetuating, but I do like to see my family when I can. Izzy always tells me that Beaulieu-Sur-Dordogne is her home now, and that's where she would like to be buried when her time comes. I say bollocks to that; if she goes before me I'm taking her bones back to England.

The food at Le Belvedere is superb, and the portions are huge. When the meals arrive all the children set to and tuck in, but I see that Izzy is pushing her salad around on the plate. I look at her and see a weariness that I remember only being there previously when our children were newly born.

"Not hungry?" I smile over at her through mouthfuls of omelette.

"Not really." She fanned herself with a menu. "It's too hot to eat."

"Perhaps an ice cream afterwards then?" I notice dark circles under her eyes that she has tried to conceal with make-up.

"Yes, that will be nice."

She is distracted and disinterested. I keep the children amused throughout the meal, all the while keeping a discreet eye on Izzy. When Solenn eventually pulls us towards the ice-cream parlour, Izzy hangs behind.

"I'll wait in the car. Can we go back soon?"

"Sure. I'll wait until they've finished eating though; I don't want ice cream on the new seats."

Marcel must be manning the security cameras; the gates open automatically as we return. Izzy has fallen asleep despite the chatter from five children at the back. Ten year old Alyce pipes up and causes Izzy to stir.

"Can we go swimming now, Grandad?"

"Wait a while and let your dinner go down." I shake my head and put the new Renault Espace into second gear down the driveway. "Let's say six o'clock for an hour before Mum and Dad come over to get you."

"Aw.....*Grandad*....." Alyce wheedles, intent on getting her own way.

Izzy half wakes up, rattles off another string of French, and all the children fall quiet. She usually only speaks English around me, and I am perturbed.

"Are you okay darling?" I bring the car to a halt outside our character stone mansion. "You don't seem yourself today."

"I'm hot, bothered and tired." Izzy is out of the car before I have turned off the engine. "I think I'll go up for a nap."

Unfortunately she doesn't make it to the front door before vomiting in the flower bed beside the porch. I signal to the children to stay in the car and call for Marie from the kitchen to keep an eye on them while I take Izzy upstairs. My wife is clearly unwell, but brushes it off with a wave of her hand.

"Too much sun. Let me sleep awhile, and I'll be fine."

The jury is out on that one. I think she may be coming down with something nasty.

CHAPTER 28

IZZY

WHEN I WAKE up I feel no better. Through the open back window I can hear the children splashing about in the pool, and realise that I need to help Ross keep an eye on them. I look at my watch; I have slept for over an hour, but still feel exhausted and nauseated. I know I need to visit a doctor, because if I admit it to myself I haven't felt well for quite a few months now.

I struggle to the toilet and the smell of my urine almost makes me want to retch again. I look down the pan; the wee is unnaturally dark, and it is the first time I have passed water all day. The evidence is looking up at me, and what with swollen ankles and my past medical training I know it all points to renal failure, but I do not want to think about having possibly inherited the kidney disease that killed my mother. I have a wonderful life here with Ross, and nothing must mar the idyll we have created for ourselves.

The heat of the day is dissipating somewhat as I put on

my bikini and matching sarong, and join Ross and the grandchildren at the pool. I feel bloated. Daisy has arrived to collect Alyce and David, but is currently lying on a sunbed chatting to Ross while the children swim up and down.

"Hi Daisy!" I wave to our daughter as I tread carefully down the steps towards the poolside. "Sorry for being so lazy; I fell asleep."

"Don't worry." Daisy smiles and looks me up and down. "You don't look well, Mum. Perhaps phone Doctor Gilbert tomorrow?"

"Yes I think I will." I nod. "It's probably a virus though."

"Anyway, it's good to get checked out, whatever it is."

Ross pipes in with his twopenn'orth, and I have a sneaky suspicion they have been talking about me in my absence. I fling off my sarong and step down into the pool, hoping the cool water will bring me out of my stupor.

By the time Laurence arrives to collect Pierre, Pascal and Solenn, I am looking forward to bedtime. Five excited children can make much noise, and my head is thumping with the effort of having to raise my voice to make myself heard. I inwardly relish the silence as I wave Laurence and Daisy off down the driveway. Ross comes to stand next to me and puts an arm around my shoulder as we watch the tail lights stop at the gate and then pass through.

"I think the kids enjoyed their day."

"Yeah" I nod. "It's great to see them, but it's even better when they all go home."

Ross chuckles and kisses my neck.

"Do you fancy an evening walk? I smell of chlorine, but

it's better than sweat."

All I want to do is curl up in bed, but I link my arm through his and we wander out down one of the interconnecting pathways. Our four acres of grounds are perfectly manicured as always, and we walk towards the old rose garden with its wooden trellis of blooms concealing a lovers' seat beneath. Ross pulls me down next to him, and I rest my head on his shoulder.

"I wonder how many people have sat here?"

"Probably hundreds." I reply, as I inhale the sweet scent of the flowers. "People just like us."

"What – filthy rich, d'you mean?" Ross laughs out loud.

"No." I nudge him with my elbow. "Couples with kids and grandkids; you know, the whole family thing." I sigh and close my eyes.

"We're so lucky Izzy. We have it all."

When I eventually reply I hear the chapel bell ringing out eight o'clock and realise I must have dozed on Ross's shoulder for at least half an hour.

"Sorry; I don't even remember falling asleep."

"This isn't like you." Ross gives my shoulder a squeeze. "I'm calling Doctor Gilbert to the house first thing in the morning."

Leon Gilbert is a trusted doctor who has been attending to our medical needs for many years. He takes one look at me and orders me to go into hospital that very afternoon for tests. I know he is right, but I don't want to admit that I am ill.

"Are you sure, Leon?" I speak to him in his native language.

"Mais oui." Leon nods and clips his bag shut.

Ross hasn't understood a word of our conversation. He sits impatiently on our Chesterfield settee waiting for Leon to depart. As soon as Marcel shows him to the door he stands squarely in front of me.

"What did he say?"

"I've got to go to hospital for tests this afternoon. I'm sure it's nothing. I'll take the Citroen and drive myself."

"You'll do no such thing." Ross shakes his head. "I'm coming with you. I've got sod all to do until the week after next when the band are coming here to discuss the next tour."

"Surely you don't need to do another one?" I look up at him in amazement. "We've got all the money we'll ever need."

"The boys still want to play; *I* need to play to keep the whole shebang going." Ross shrugs. "It's all I *can* do."

We make the trip to the hospital in silence, each thinking our own thoughts. All that runs through my head is the sight of my mother in the last weeks of her life. I'm not sure if Ross remembers much about that time, but it's still as clear in my mind as yesterday. As Ross drives into town a little too fast, I hope and pray to the dear Lord above that I am not going to have to crawl on my hands and knees to ask my estranged sister if she would like to donate one of her kidneys.

In the various departments I am subjected to a barrage of scans, and blood and urine tests. Then, scared witless, I have to wait patiently in my hospital bed to find out the results and to discover just what the future has in store for me.

CHAPTER 29

CLARE

WHEN I GET home from work I glance again at the unopened envelope I left sitting on the hall table earlier that morning. I know the handwriting, which is why I am hesitant to investigate further. The scrawl is my sister's; I would recognise it anywhere. In the end it is James who hands the envelope to me later that evening after dinner when Lauren and Matty are out, but I ask him to open it and read it through. However, when he has skimmed over it, he shakes his head and gives it back to me.

"You'd best read this; it's from Izzy."

My heart sinks at the confirmation. With reluctance I take it from him and begin to read:

Maison Tyler
95664 Beaulieu Sur Dordogne
France

24th September 2002

Dear Clare,

I hope you don't mind, but I asked Rachel for your address. I know you still cannot forgive me for taking Ross away from you, and I totally understand. Although Ross and I have been very happy together, a part of me died with the knowledge that I was to blame for hurting you so much. Can you ever see your way to forgive me? After 30 years I need my sister like never before.

Clare, I do not know who else to turn to. I am desperately ill with kidney failure. Like Mum they found I was born with only one kidney, and I am now in end stage renal failure. I am on the list for a transplant, but donors are scarce.

I know what I am asking from you is huge, but unless I receive a kidney transplant I will die, just like Mum did. At the moment my options are limited and donors are scarce. Please reply to the address above and let us get to know each other again before it's too late.

All my love,
Izzy x

"What does she mean when she said she took Ross away from you?"

I am brought out of my stupor by James, who is looking at me accusingly. I shake my head.

"Leave it; it's all water under the bridge."

Unfortunately my words only serve to inflame him further. He refuses to let the matter rest.

"Were you and Ross together before he married Izzy then?"

I sigh and nod.

"Yes, but only for a short time. As you can see from the

letter, he and Izzy fell in love."

"Why did you never say anything about it?"

I can hear the hurt in his voice. The last thing I want is to cause him any pain.

"It was all over before I met you. Please James, I don't want to talk about it anymore."

"But *I* want to talk about it!" His voice rises in pitch. "Jesus Clare, he's your brother-in-law!"

"I know, but I haven't seen him for decades. Forget it." I slam the letter down on the table. "It's over."

"So *that's* why you and your sister never speak!" James glares at me. "I always wondered what the reason was. Why did you never tell me?"

"Do I ever ask you about your former girlfriends? Come on, be reasonable!" I face him across the kitchen table. "There are some things in life that need to remain private."

"But not from your partner!" James stands up and runs a hand through his hair in frustration. "What are you going to do? Are you going to meet up with him again? What's going on?"

I stand up, walk around the table towards him, and slide my arms around his back.

"Nothing's going on. Obviously Izzy is ill, but it's got nothing to do with me. She can't expect me to rush to her aid after all this time. She took my boyfriend; I got over that years ago and met you. We've got two lovely children. I don't know how she's got the nerve to write; what does she expect me to do? Willingly give her one of my kidneys? Knowing her she'll want both of them anyway." I lay my head on James's chest. "Don't worry; I'm going to tear the letter up."

With James mollified we wash up the dinner things in a kind of companionable silence. However, in the back of my mind is the picture of Izzy dying somewhere in a French hospital bed surrounded by drips and tubes. I push the vision from my mind; I don't suppose I would recognise my sister now even if she suddenly recovered enough to knock on my front door. The chasm between us is unbridgeable, forged by years of silence. We are two different people than the empty-headed girls we once were. I decide to have a word with Rachel and let her know that I definitely do not want any more contact from Isabel, Ross, or any of their family.

I always hate October. The nights start drawing in, reminding me that all there is to look forward to is five or six months of cold weather. I am the first to arrive home on the last Friday before half term and I am irritated to see that a hired car has parked right across our driveway, preventing me from parking outside the house. I can see somebody sitting in the driver's seat, and so I pull up behind the black BMW and get out of my car, hoping the expression on my face is enough for the driver to register my displeasure.

A man steps out as I walk towards the BMW. He is wearing jeans, a light sweatshirt, and a baseball cap and sunglasses, even though the day is overcast. As he looks at me the years fall away, for although he is obviously older and has put on a little weight, I would recognise that smile anywhere.

"Hey, babe."

He takes off his baseball cap to reveal shoulder-length fair hair with only a touch of grey. I am momentarily stunned, and blurt out the only thing I can think of at that precise moment.

    "Hello Ross."

CHAPTER 30

IZZY

ALL I WANT to be is normal like everybody else. I *hate* being stuck on a dialysis machine three times a week; the muscle cramps are horrendous. I feel sick and permanently tired. Why has this happened to me? Am I being punished for my past sins? Clare would say I am, I'm sure.

I sent the letter weeks ago. Every day I hope for a reply, but there is none. I know I sent it to the right address; Rachel wouldn't have given me an old one. Ross checked the tracking, and it was delivered. *Why doesn't she reply?* Time is running out for me.

Now I know what Mum had to suffer. I feel guilty now because I was too busy with my own life to give her the attention she needed at the time. All this time I never knew I only had one kidney, just like her. As a very last resort Paul has offered to donate, but with three children to look after as well as acting CEO of Ross's business empire, I would feel terrible putting any pressure on him with the big anniversary tour coming up. I know Laurence would not want him to go through such a major operation either. It is so difficult. Daisy would lay down her life for me, but has taken after Ross and is not a match.

I can tell by looking in my husband's eyes that he is worried sick. I tend to lay about and let things all go over my head these days due to the fatigue, but I know when he is fretting. Before he flew to Gatwick this morning he kissed me and said how he had to go to London on business. Does he think I'm stupid? Rachel told me he asked for Clare's address. I know for certain that business or no business, he will not fly home again until he has seen her.

Is she still pretty? I look like an old woman of 90. My skin is a horrible sickly colour. My hair is thin and brittle. Perhaps a visit to the hairdresser will cheer me up; it always used to make me feel better, but unfortunately nothing will really aid me now except a transplant.

I am only 54 years of age. Too young really to think about dying. I still have a whole lot of living to do, not to mention watching my grandchildren grow up. Dear little Solenn is my favourite. I know we shouldn't have favourites, but sometimes you just have a feeling for a child that will not go away. Solenn is as bright as a button; I feel there's a bond between us that will only grow stronger as time marches on.

How much time do I have? I suppose that's a question none of us know the answer to. All we can do is try to keep our bodies as healthy as possible until the day the Grim Reaper catches up with us. Unfortunately I feel my time on earth is more limited than most. This knowledge makes me want to cram in as much living as I can in whatever time I have left. I want to untie the hands that are metaphorically manacled behind my back, in order to reach for the moon.

I want. I want. I want. Mum always used to tell me that want doesn't get.

CHAPTER 31

ROSS

SHE DOESN'T LOOK bad at all, considering she must be about fifty by now. Her hair is short and cut into layers, and looks as if it has recently had a new coat of light brown paint. I quickly put my baseball cap back on in case I'm recognised by any passers-by.

"It's good to see you again, Clare. Why live in Suffolk though? It's the arse end of nowhere."

"*We* like it."

She stands looking at me as though she's made of stone. I often have this effect on fans, but I thought Clare might have been made of sterner stuff.

"Can I come in? Word will get out that I'm here in a minute, and you won't be able to get out of your front door for all the ladders in the way."

"Ladders?" She smiles at me but still looks blank.

"So the Press can see in your bedroom windows."

"Oh God". She speaks at last. "Sorry, do come in. It's been such a long time."

I'm aware that she cannot take her eyes off me. I let her go in front, and follow her into the garden. She unlocks the door to one of those suburban semis which were built in the 1930's; solid with a bay window at the front and pebble dashed walls, and then turns around to look at me again.

"Come in; are you over here for long?"

"No; I just need to speak to you about Izzy. I'm getting the plane back to Laroche tonight."

An inscrutable expression comes over her face when I mention her sister. She ushers me into her front room and points towards a long curved cream-coloured settee that takes up one corner.

"Do sit down. Can I get you a drink? Beer? Coffee?"

"A beer would be great. Thanks."

I take a moment to look around while she goes to the kitchen. The room is functional with solid pine furniture, but there's nothing that particularly stands out. A few family photos catch my eye, and I'm drawn to Clare's wedding picture above the mantelpiece. Her face has the beautiful bloom of youth that I remember, but she has a kind of faraway look as she stands in close to her husband. I have a sudden egocentric thought: *Was she thinking about me at the time?*

I hear footsteps coming back up the hallway, and she reappears clutching a can of beer and a half pint glass.

"Thanks." I take the beer from her. "I suppose you know why I'm here."

"Not really."

The tone of her voice says otherwise. She knows exactly why I've come.

"Did you get Izzy's letter?"

"No."

She shakes her head and I don't believe her for one minute.

"The tracking says it was delivered."

She shrugs and looks away as a key turns in the front door.

"That'll be James and Matty. James teaches at Matty's school."

A boy of about 15 or 16 runs in, but stops when he sees me. This is the first time I have laid eyes on my nephew. He favours his father in looks. I stand up and offer out my right hand.

"Hello; I'm your uncle Ross."

The boy looks momentarily stunned, as most people do when they see me for the first time. Sometimes I wonder if I have two heads, but then I realise they've probably just seen my mug in the newspapers, especially after that court case finished with Parlaphone.

"I'm Matty."

He shakes my hand just as his father comes into the room. I've only heard about James through Rachel; who has portrayed him as kind and hard-working. I turn from the boy to his father.

"Hi; I'm Ross, Izzy's husband."

James doesn't seem too pleased to see me. He shakes my hand with a firm, warm grip.

"I suppose you've come because of the letter?"

I see a flash of anger shoot from Clare to James. I pretend not to notice and take a sip of beer.

"Yes. I need to talk to Clare about it."

"Be my guest; Matty and I will make ourselves scarce."

When Clare and I are alone I finish up the beer and wonder how on earth I can broach the real subject of why I came.

"Izzy doesn't know I'm here."

"I figured *that* one out."

She gives a short laugh and I am momentarily taken back to the heat of a day long past where a young girl with a face like an angel devours my last apple and allows the juice to run carelessly down her chin, such was her need of the fruit.

"She's sick, Clare; really sick. She needs a kidney transplant."

"And this is where I come in, I expect."

The tone of her voice is cold and unfeeling. I decide to play a trump card. It might work, or it might not.

"Paul could donate so don't think the pressure is totally on you, but he's a busy lawyer and runs my business side of things. It would be really difficult for him to take the time off at the moment, with another tour coming up. Plus the fact he has three little kids. All I can say is name your price, Clare. Under the circumstances I can't expect you to donate a kidney to Izzy without some sort of financial reward. Would you like your mortgage paid off? A bigger house? Name it, and it's yours."

"With two children to bring up we've never been able to afford the deposit for a mortgage. The house is rented. Rachel, as Dad's wife, inherited his estate when he died intestate with Alzheimer's, but I never really got on with her. She kept his money out of spite, I think."

"There you go then. I'll buy you and James a house, a

fucking *big* house. What do you say? Is it a yes? By the look of Izzy at the moment, she won't make old bones at this rate. I love her, Clare, and I'll love you for the rest of my life if you can do this one thing for your sister."

I can almost see the cogs going around and around in her head as she weighs up the pros and cons. Finally she gives me one of those dazzling smiles I remember so well, and nods.

"I'll do it."

I'm not sure if she's decided to do it for me or Izzy, but I'm so exhilarated I don't know what to do. Even doing a line of coke or cooking up some brown sugar is not as good as this. Instinctively I let out a whooping noise, pick her up in my arms, and twirl her around. She throws her head back and laughs out loud just as her husband comes back into the room with a face like a smacked arse.

CHAPTER 32

JAMES

I DON'T QUITE know what's going on here, but suddenly my wife is singing in the shower and investigating large houses that are for sale in London, while preparing to fly off to France next week at *his* expense. *He* seems to have taken over her every waking thought, making me wonder if this romance that I never knew existed has re-surfaced and will be continued when he picks her up at Laroche airport. She's asked for special leave after half-term to stay in France to recover from the transplant, and I'll be left here with the kids to keep everything ticking over.

I feel shut out. I don't want to be beholden to that wanker for the rest of my life. I resent him coming into our house and flashing his money about. It's got nothing to do with Clare wanting to help her sister whom she hasn't spoken to for years; he's bowled her over with his good looks and his expensive lifestyle. How am I going to furnish a bloody mansion on my salary? She doesn't think of that aspect of it;

the council tax and the heating bills will probably take a month's wages on their own. She earns peanuts; it just won't work.

Nothing was discussed with me; she just announced it as a *fait accompli*. She is going to have the tests next week to make sure her kidney is a perfect match, and then she'll have the operation probably on Wednesday of the following week. I'm just supposed to shut up and accept it all.

Lauren cried when we dropped Clare off at Gatwick this evening. She doesn't want her mum to lose a kidney. Why doesn't Izzy's son have the op instead? Matt seems rather stoic about the whole thing, but I suppose that's because he's a boy. I tend to agree with Lauren. What if her one remaining kidney starts to fail when she's older? What if the transplanted kidney doesn't work and her sister dies anyway? She doesn't seem to have considered these problems at all. Kidney failure is obviously in her family; she's letting her heart rule her head.

She phoned my mobile when she arrived at Laroche. I could hear him in the background barking out orders to some poor sod and interrupting when I was trying to talk to her. *Bastard.* In my opinion they could have waited a bit longer for a donor; sooner or later one would have surfaced, I'm sure. I suppose with all his money he's used to getting what he wants *when* he wants it.

All I've had this evening are phone calls from estate agents rubbing their hands together with glee at the thought of two per cent commission on a £750,000 house. I never knew there were so many mansions up for sale. Of course she wants one with a swimming pool; the trouble is where is the money going to come from to maintain it? Will the rock star pay our electric bill for heating the water? As I used to say to Clare when the kids played up at the end of the day – there'll be tears before bedtime at this rate.

After nearly a week I'm missing Clare like crazy. She's phoned to say all the test results are coming back positive. She's having counselling today to make sure she still wants to go through with it. With a bit of luck she might change her mind, although she seems a perfect match for her sister, as I thought she probably would be. She's a bit cagey when she phones, as I suspect *he's* listening in, and so we both just keep to general chit-chat. As far as I can tell she's staying there at the house with him. After learning of their past romance I don't like it a bit, but I'm powerless to do anything about it this far away and with work commitments as they are.

I am worried for Clare's future. I know she will have the best care for the 3 or 4 days while she recovers from the operation, but she will still be left with only one kidney. I have started Googling kidney donors and transplants in the evenings. I realise the body can function adequately with only one kidney, but I still wish Clare did not have to go through this. Apparently as a donor she would be placed at the top of the waiting list if her remaining kidney started to fail, but who's to say one will ever become available? The most likely scenario would be that it would be down to Lauren or Matty to be tested, but I know Clare would never submit either of them to major surgery on her behalf.

I have to stop worrying about things I cannot control. My wife sees a better future for our family if she undergoes the operation, but I am happy with our little home and hate having to kowtow to my brother-in-law. I am realistic and practical, whereas Clare tends to act before she thinks. Ross will ensure I have to be forever grateful for his largesse, and the more I think on it the more I realise that this new lifestyle will not work as we will be living well above our means.

I tried to ask Clare about how she's getting on with Isabel after all this time, but she skirted around the issue. Most people would be doing all this for the love of their sister, but with my wife I rather think that the love of Ross and money is at the forefront of her actions. Perhaps she knows something I don't, but unless the rock star augments our income on a permanent basis I can see us selling the house before we've even moved in.

Another subject she's avoiding is her previous relationship with Ross. What's happening with him? Have they rekindled an old love? Is he showing her how grateful he is in ways other than monetary? I feel literally *impotent*. I need to take some sick leave, get Rachel here to keep an eye on Matty, and go and find out what the hell's going on.

CHAPTER 33

CLARE

UP UNTIL NOW I've been busy with all the tests, scans and counselling, and have actually managed to put off going into Izzy's side room. Ross has told her I'm the donor, but said to me yesterday that today would be a good day for me to visit her following my last counselling session, because she would have had dialysis overnight. I don't want to see her, but Ross tells me that she needs and wishes to say thanks.

The clock by my bed says 07:45. I am wide awake and looking around at the opulence of the guest room. My four poster bed is perched on a kind of plinth. I swing my legs over the side of the bed and walk down a few steps, which are carpeted in white shag pile. The same light, luxurious carpet covers the entire room, which to my untrained eye must measure at least 25 feet by 20 feet. I leave footsteps in the carpet as I walk. There are two empty walk-in wardrobes, and a Jacuzzi as well as a shower, toilet and bidet in the en-suite bathroom. White crushed velvet curtains drape the windows, and I pull them apart to let in the daylight.

The grounds stretch out before me. Already I can see a team of gardeners at work, cutting, pruning and snipping. My sister obviously wants for nothing in this gated complex of hers.

On one of the paths criss-crossing the grounds I can see Ross out for an early morning jog. He has donned a grey tracksuit, and wears earphones attached to what looks like one of the new iPods clipped around his waist. His trainers beat out a regular rhythm on the path, and he waves to one of the gardeners, who raises his right hand in an answering greeting.

As he runs back towards the house I watch the movement of his hair, and notice the well-developed musculature beneath the folds of his tracksuit. As though sensing my presence, he looks up and waves. Embarrassed that he has discovered me standing there in my nightdress staring at him, I quickly move away.

Showered and clad in more suitable attire I emerge onto the second floor galleried landing. From the domed glass ceiling down through to the first floor landing hangs a large central chandelier, and a grand staircase running two floors down to the main tiled hallway adds to the property's opulence. The house is quiet at this time of the day, but Ross seems to be an early riser now and I know that he will already be waiting for me down in the breakfast room.

Holding onto the bannister with one hand I swan down the stairs with as much elegance as I can muster on an empty stomach. I feel as though I should be making a grand entrance to swathes of adoring people, but there is nobody at the foot of the staircase as I turn right and walk along through the kitchen to the sunny breakfast room where Ross sits eating a mushroom omelette.

"Morning!" He chirps, with a face full of omelette. "It's all laid out on the side there. Help yourself."

I lift up the lids of the silver serving dishes.

"Goodness! Is this all just for us two?"

"Apparently. Even *I* think Marie has gone overboard this morning."

He smiles, and I try and think of James at home waiting for me to return. It doesn't work, because all I can see is Ross. I help myself to an omelette, sausages and tomatoes, and seat myself in the chair opposite him.

"You have the most wonderful house."

"All Izzy's work regarding the décor and furnishings. All I did was pay for it."

He manages to bring Izzy into every facet of the conversation. Nervousness at seeing her later in the day starts to gnaw at my stomach, and I find I cannot eat much.

"Not hungry?" He starts on one of his four sausages. "The food isn't that good in the hospital canteen."

"I'm just a bit nervous at seeing Izzy again."

"Not as nervous as she is about seeing *you*." Ross laughs and pours some tea. "She had the hairdressers in last night."

"Oh, God." I roll my eyes heavenwards. "Am I that scary?"

"She seems to think so. She thinks you're going to start shouting at her."

I mask my surprise at his words and sip some tea.

"It's all in the past. I have my own family now. We have to move on, don't we?"

"Of course." He nods in agreement. "That's what I said to her."

I nibble at a sausage to hide my disappointment.

The staff at the private hospital are quietly efficient, as they silently bustle about their business. My heart is hammering away in my chest as I approach Izzy's room. I let Ross go in front, and wish I was anywhere else except my present location; even sitting in the dentist's chair having my teeth drilled would be preferable to this.

As I walk into the room I receive a jolt of shock and surprise. If I hadn't known it was my sister in the bed, I would have thought it was my mother in the last stages of her illness. Gone were the sultry good looks, the long shiny black hair, and model figure. Instead in their place was a thin middle aged woman with a greyish, lined complexion and a short dyed bob, who hobbled out of her armchair with difficulty at the sight of me.

"Clare! It's so lovely to see you!"

I was so stunned at the likeness to Mum, that I was momentarily lost for words. Ross looked from me to Izzy.

"I'll leave you two girls in peace and go and find a cup of coffee. I'll be back in about half an hour."

I saw the look of love pass between them, and felt an utter fool for ever thinking that Ross might want to come back to me. Izzy nodded and smiled at him, leaving me to break the silence between us as he left and closed the door behind him.

"Hello Izzy." I stood there awkwardly, not knowing what to say.

"Come and sit down." Izzy waved me towards a visitor's

chair. "I don't know how to thank you for agreeing to all this. I take it Ross has offered you compensation?"

"Yes; he's been very generous. We are still renting, and he has offered to buy us a house."

"Good." Izzy nodded. "Rachel phoned and told us you're not homeowners."

"But Ross offered to pay our mortgage!"

"He probably didn't want to let on that he'd spoken to Rachel."

A wave of irritation washed through me at the sound of our stepmother's name.

"What else has she been saying?"

"Nothing much." Izzy shrugged. "He asked her if you were renting because I wanted to thank you in some way for giving me the chance to see my grandchildren grow up. I've hardly been the perfect sister to you, and you turn around and do this wonderful thing for me. It just goes some way to assuage my feelings of guilt."

I remained silent. It seemed too soon to mention all that had gone on in the past. I was suddenly on a massive guilt trip myself, harbouring thoughts that if Ross had not turned up on my doorstep offering me money I would have let my sister die. I had done this all for Ross, but seeing Izzy so frail and vulnerable in a hospital bed brought home to me the fact that my lack of action would, in my opinion, have made me almost as bad as any murderer running loose in the streets with a machine gun.

I hung my head so that she would not see my eyes fill with tears. My sister fell in love with her soul mate, a man who loves her so much he will try moving heaven and earth in his efforts to keep her alive. I had loved him too, and the fact that I had mistakenly considered him *my* soul mate had kept Izzy and me apart for more than 30 years. But what business did I ever have with trying to split them up? Ross had never been anything other than a perfect gentleman to me. However, now I was here I could see that the love between them would fire their hearts for the rest of their lives and beyond. Mine was an unrequited love that would always have to stay precisely that.

At that moment in time I absolutely hated myself.

CHAPTER 34

JAMES

I *HAVE TO* see my wife. Lauren has been a brick about getting Matty to school, and I must repay her in some way. Clare gave me their address just in case; I *have* to go to his house and see for myself that nothing is going on between them. The thought that my wife is sleeping under his roof for another night at least before the operation is starting to twist my guts up into knots.

The M25 is playing its usual orbital car park game. After a while the red tail lights start to hurt my eyes as black clouds descend; thank goodness I left plenty of time to get to Gatwick. As I reach the airport, the South terminal's summer parking sign looks slightly ironic in the pissing rain, and I turn my wipers on full in order to catch the number of the zone where I need to drive to.

There's another family parking a 10 year old Mondeo as I ease into the adjoining space; Mum, Dad and two bored looking teenage boys. Pretty soon my own teenage son is going to have to cope with a major upheaval if Clare insists on moving us all into some preposterous mansion. The whole idea is absurd; it is not *us*. We are ordinary people, unused to life's luxuries except for the odd meal out on a Saturday night or some tickets to see Ipswich play.

I pick up my overnight bag and make a dash for the bus shelter. The rain is unrelenting, perfect for my miserable, melancholic mood. The family of four stand behind me in the queue, buoyed up despite the weather. As I step on the courtesy bus I try and sit as far away from them as possible.

Gatwick I think is one of my least favourite airports, but it was the only one which had an available flight to Laroche at the time I needed to go. I find the check-in desk and join the queue. There is an hour and a half before the flight. If I have to sit next to a screaming toddler on the plane I think I might not be responsible for my actions.

When I have satisfied the security staff at the entrance to the departure lounge that I am not carrying any explosives in my shoes or a gun in my back pocket, I am free to wander around the ridiculously overpriced shops. Should I take Clare a present? Some perfume? Would she question my motives if I turn up carrying a bottle of Chanel No 5? He's probably using gallons of it as bath oil anyway. I have a sudden mental picture of both of them naked and entwined in one of his hot tubs. I decide against the perfume and turn away.

I'm too keyed up to settle down and read a newspaper. What I would really like to do is join the smokers in the little glass box room I have noticed over to one side. I haven't smoked for years, but I have a sudden craving for nicotine. Feeling like a naughty schoolboy I buy ten cigarettes, trying not to notice the picture of some poor sod's lung cancer on the front of the packet. I know I'll only get to smoke one or two and will have to throw away the rest of them away, but their instant calming effect is the one I'm after now; the lung cancer can go to hell.

As I open the smoking room door I realise I don't have a lighter. There are two other smokers in there puffing away trying to loosen their load; one is an attractive brunette and the other is an overweight businessman in a grey suit. I approach the suit, as the last thing I need is some young woman thinking I'm going to start chatting her up.

As the nicotine fumes hit the back of my throat I could almost cry with relief. I sit down in a comfortable armchair and watch the people in the departure lounge scurrying to and fro like worker ants on a mission. I know Clare's nose will probably pick up on my new tobacco scent, but I'll think up a probable explanation if and when the situation occurs.

After the second cigarette I am more laid back than Val Doonican on Diazepam. I see the gate number come up on the screen, ditch the rest of the cigarettes in the bin, and make my way out of the departure lounge, feeling more able to face my foe.

It's a good eight degrees warmer at Laroche. I make sure my hired Fiat has a satnav, and enter in the destination. It's about a 45 minute mainly motorway drive, but I need that time to prepare for what I might come across when I arrive there.

When I reach Beaulieu I am impressed at the medieval town with its narrow cobbled streets, market area, and pleasant gardens. The directions steer me away from the centre of the town with its variety of shops and up a long tree-lined hill. At the top of the hill I am surprised to find that Ross and Izzy are living in a gated and walled compound. There is a security phone to the right of a rather forbiddingly high closed gate.

"Hello." I speak timidly into the phone. "I am James McVie, Clare's husband."

"They are at the 'opital." A heavily accented male voice comes down the line.

"Is it possible to wait, please?"

"I 'ave no orders to let you in."

"Then I'll wait here. If it's possible to have a drink I'd be grateful. Thanks."

No drink arrives, and I edge the car a little way back onto the road. I want to watch them as they come back in.

They do not strike me as a typical couple in love as a silver left-hand drive Jaguar comes up the hill towards me. Clare isn't speaking at all, and is looking idly out of the passenger window. I see Ross checking me out, but then Clare recognises me and breaks into a smile. He stops the car and she jumps out and runs over towards where I am parked.

"James! What are you doing here?"

I am so happy to see my wife that I leap out of the car and enfold her in my arms in the middle of the road, oblivious to Ross looking on from inside the Jag.

"I just wanted to be with you."

"Who's looking after Matty?"

"Lauren's going to run him to school before she goes to work, and Rachel is going to bring him home. Don't worry, it's all under control."

"The op's going to be tomorrow. It's my last night here. Ross has been great."

I don't want to think about how wonderful Ross has been. I want to scoop my wife up and tear back to the airport with her at double speed.

"Hi James, how's it going?"

Ross has walked over to where we are standing. His right hand is outstretched. I shake it with my own, and keep one arm proprietorially around Clare.

"It's not going too well at the moment; your staff wouldn't let me in. I've been sitting here for ages."

"Sorry about that. You should have let us know you were coming."

"It was a spur of the moment thing."

"Follow me in and park next to mine."

The gate opens as we stand there. Clare disentangles herself from me and jumps in the Fiat.

"Come on James; tell me what's been going on at home."

I am with my wife, where I am meant to be. My heart returns to its normal rhythm and I start up the car, much happier than when I had left Gatwick. Clare's nose wrinkles as she closes the door.

"Have you been smoking? It stinks in here."

"I sat next to a smoker on the plane." "Oh."

CHAPTER 35

CLARE

I WAS NOT in the least surprised when I saw James waiting outside. It's just the sort of thing he would do. He was obviously imagining Ross and me making passionate love on the patio, in the swimming pool, or under the satin sheets. The scent of tobacco clings to his shirt; he probably needed a couple of ciggies at the airport to stop himself from getting so worked up. I must admit that the thought of having sex with Ross is not totally unpleasant, but I am coming to terms with the reality that he is, always has been, and always will be in love with my sister. I feel rather stupid to think that I've had a sort of unrequited schoolgirl crush on him for all this time, but he *was* my first love, and you never forget those powerful emotions do you? However, if I stop to analyse myself, I think the person I've been in love with for years is the golden boy who rescued me from Desolation Hill back in 1970. He's long gone now, and I need to stop thinking about him and focus more on my own relationship, and realise what a good man I have in James.

There's not much time to chat before we arrive at the house. Marcel runs out into the courtyard full of apologies, but Ross smooths things over and tells him he did the right thing. I hear James complaining that he is parched, and Marcel immediately brings some ice cold beer into the hallway as the three of us stand there.

"Thank you." James takes a glass from Marcel. "This'll hit the spot."

Ross takes a beer and offers me the same, but I shake my head. He looks at James and smiles.

"I have to be very security conscious I'm afraid. We quite often get some real weirdos hanging around outside."

"I appreciate that." James nods. "I was prepared to wait. I missed my wife."

I feel embarrassed, knowing the real reason he came here.

"I'll be home before you know it. The op is tomorrow, and so I'm going to stuff myself silly at dinner tonight. Nil by mouth sucks."

"Izzy can't eat much, but they'll give her dinner at the hospital tonight anyway." Ross sighed. "It'll be nice to see her putting on a few pounds after all this is over. Clare, why don't you show James around? He'd also probably like a shower before dinner; I'll ask Marie to bring some more towels to your room." Ross drained his glass. "Excuse me for a while; I just have to make a couple of phone calls."

"Sure." I nod at Ross. "Come on James, I'll give you a little tour."

When we eventually reach the privacy of our room, James

closes the door, wraps his arms around me, and sighs. "Are you sure you still want to go through with this?"

"Perfectly sure." I nod my head against his chest. "The only way it will affect me is some pain afterwards and not being able to lift anything heavy for six weeks. However, Izzy's sick; I can't let my sister die. I went to see her yesterday for the first time in over thirty years. I've had a chance to do some serious thinking; it's what I want to do."

"But what if anything happens to your one remaining kidney?"

I pull back from him a bit, and look him straight in the eye.

"Don't worry; I've read it'll grow in size to compensate and have at least a seventy five per cent increase in function."

"How the fuck will it know it's the only kidney left? Will one of them shout out to the other one across the backbone to say it's going away on a little holiday or something?"

I giggle, but I sense James' frustration. I shrug my shoulders.

"Yeah, it'll say 'Keep my seat warm, but don't bust your pooper while I'm away'. Who knows? That's one of the wonders of the body isn't it? It *will* happen though; I'll lead a perfectly normal life."

"What happens if Izzy doesn't recover? You'd have lost a kidney for nothing. Will they be able to transplant it back in?"

I realise James is desperately worried, but try to allay his fears.

"Probably not, as they'll be scar tissue and damage to it from surgery, and my other one would have already enlarged anyway."

He is not about to give up. As he throws off his clothes

and heads for the shower he has one last question.

"Why doesn't someone else from her own immediate family help out? Why has it got to be *you*?"

I stand at the door of the en-suite and watch as naked and disgruntled, he steps into the shower.

"Her grandchildren are too young, her daughter has Ross's blood group, and her son is busy organising a world tour for the band and has three little children to look after. He has to stay fit. I've grown up. Please support me; it's now something I *want* to do."

"Well, *I* don't want you to do it." He stares at me through the glass.

"I'm sorry James, but it *will* go ahead tomorrow."

He turns his back on me and wrestles with the French plumbing.

"Cheers for considering my point of view."

I go back into the bedroom and flop down on the bed, disappointed beyond measure.

"Marie has excelled herself tonight. This beef is delicious."

I help myself to more roast potatoes and haricot beans. James is morose as he plays with his food. I am sure Ross has picked up on the atmosphere as he pours himself more wine and lifts his glass."

"Let's hope we will have two successful operations tomorrow."

I clink my glass of water with his. James reluctantly raises his pint of beer.

"Yeah, let's hope. My wife's doing a great thing for Izzy here."

"And you've no idea how much I appreciate it."   Ross

looks at me. "Here's what I promised you."

He brings a piece of paper out of his pocket and extends his hand towards me. I put my glass down and take the paper from his grasp, unable to stop my hand from shaking as I realise it's a cheque for two million pounds. I notice the Swiss bank account, tomorrow's date, and the fact that our names are written on the 'Pay' line.

"This is too, too generous Ross." I shake my head and try to give it back. "I cannot accept this."

"Yes you can, and you must. You are doing something wonderful for Izzy and me, and I want to compensate you in the best way I know how. It's a mere bagatelle for me; I don't want to boast too much, but don't forget I'm up there with the Paul McCartneys of this world."

I stare at the cheque for some considerable time before passing it to James. We look at each other in disbelief. Finally James finds his voice, stands up, and extends his hand across the huge oak dining table towards Ross.

"*Now* who's the one doing something wonderful? This is a dream come true for us. I don't know how to thank you. This is way beyond what we ever expected."

"One good turn deserves another, so they say. Invite Izzy and me to your new house sometime. That will be thanks enough."

Ross and James shake hands, and humbled and ashamed, I am left close to tears at the generosity of a man with not an ounce of bitterness or hatred in his body for suffering more than thirty years of my crass behaviour towards his wife, his Izzy, the love of his privileged, charmed life.

CHAPTER 36

ROSS

THEY WOULD BE appalled to know I heard them making love as I crept upstairs last night. To be able to make such a difference in their lives gives me a great kick, although they don't need to know how much I'm really worth. Paul tells me it's close to 700 million pounds. He's the lawyer with Izzy's brain power, and so I have to believe him. All I need to do is write hit singles and sing; he deals with the rest. It works well for both of us.

I switch the alarm off before it blares out again, and check my phone on the bedside cabinet. There is a text from Izzy saying that she is awake and more excited than she has been in ages, despite not being able to eat or drink anything. I smile as I picture the healthy beautiful woman that she once was, and the one she will become again.

Above my head the floorboards creak. Clare and James are preparing for the big day already. I sit up, swing my legs over the side of the bed, rub my eyes, and then stand up and head for the shower. Have I got time for a toke to calm the nerves? I remembered at the last minute to ask Marie to bring my breakfast up to my room this morning. I don't want to eat in front of Clare, who obviously must be nil by mouth and doesn't need to be assaulted by the aroma of fried bacon rolls. I managed to get out of James that he doesn't eat breakfast anyway. Perhaps *I* shouldn't? The waist is somewhat larger than it used to be.

When I hear them walking downstairs from the guest room I come out onto the landing. Clare looks a little nervous, but that's completely understandable.

"Morning! Ready to rock?"

"Am I ever!"

Clare smiles at me and I join them on the stairs, taking her hospital bag from James, and giving it to Marcel to put in the car.

"We're a little early, but it's better to be early than late." I check my phone.

"Let's just get it over with."

Thank goodness Clare has not changed her mind. I walk a little too hurriedly to the car, and take the keys from Marcel.

"Bonne chance M'sieu."

"Merci."

It's the only French word I'm happy saying. Anything else just sounds so *wrong* when it comes out of my mouth, unlike the molten silk when Izzy speaks. I need to keep my wife alive if only to tell me what the hell everybody's talking about.

The hospital car park is virtually empty at this time of day. The three of us haven't spoken much since we left the house.

When we reach the reception desk there is another surprise for Clare; the staff have moved Izzy to a double room, and Izzy points out an empty bed alongside hers as we arrive.

"Here's your bed, Clare. When we're both awake later we can have a good old chat."

I kiss my wife, noticing that Clare seems inordinately pleased at being able to share with her sister. James fetches some visitor chairs, and the four of us sit looking at each other expectantly. Izzy is the first to speak.

"I'm feeling better than I have for ages; it must be the adrenalin."

"I'm nervous, but okay." Clare shakes her head. "I still can't get over the fact that Ross gave us a cheque for two million pounds last night."

"Believe it." Izzy laughs. "It's what we both wanted to do."

We are interrupted by a nurse entering to admit Clare and for both girls to sign consent forms. Then an anaesthetist appears in a white coat to check both Izzy and Clare over. It's a busy room all of a sudden, with the surgeon appearing for a chat as well. Thankfully he speaks good English, as he first looks at Clare and then at Izzy.

"I am M'sieu Bertrand. I will just explain the procedure to you. Madame McVie, we will dissect your kidney via laparoscopic surgery. You are lucky now to only need a small incision just above the pubic bone for removal of the kidney. In years gone by we would have needed to remove a rib and you would have had a long scar which obviously would have taken more time to heal. Madame Tyler, we will not remove your present kidney, but will just attach your sister's through an incision in your lower abdomen. We will then attach blood vessels from your lower abdomen to the kidney, and then attach the ureter, which will probably need a small stent for the first six weeks or so to improve the flow of urine. Madame Tyler, your operation will take about three hours, and Madame McVie's about two hours. You will both have catheters on waking to monitor urine output, and morphine drips for pain. Do you understand the procedures?"

"Yes." Clare and Izzy both affirm simultaneously.

"No lifting for both of you for six weeks after surgery, and *bien sur* there will be follow up appointments. If you have signed the consent forms, then we are ready to go. Please could you change into your hospital gowns and await the porters."

James and I give the girls their privacy and wait outside while they undress. It looks as though this stranger, my brother-in-law, is going to be my sole companion for the next few hours. He sighs and paces up and down the corridor.

"I could sure do with a cigarette." "Me too, but you can't smoke in here."

"I know, but it doesn't stop me wanting one."

He's a nervous bundle of energy. I'm going to have my work cut out keeping him calm. I'm glad I found time for a joint before we came out. Clare opens the door wearing a dressing gown over one of those abominable hospital robe things that offers a patient no dignity from the back. She walks over to James and they begin chatting. I take the opportunity to go back in and speak to Izzy alone.

My wife looks tired even before the operation begins. I kiss her forehead and take her hands in mine.

"Well, this is what we've been waiting for."

"I'm so nervous." Izzy exhales slowly and closes her

eyes. "They've given me a shot of immunosuppressive already."

"You won't know anything about it. When you wake up it'll all be over."

"Thank God." She nods slightly. "I never thought I'd see this day. I thought I'd be dead by now, like Mum."

"Your mum never took care of her condition. You're not going anywhere. You've got to stay alive; I can't understand a bloody word of French."

"The anti-rejection drugs are going to make me susceptible to infection. I can't be around lots of germy people now."

"You won't be. I'll see to that."

I stroke her hair, and her eyes stay closed. Pretty soon she falls into a fitful doze, and is still asleep when the porters arrive to take both girls to their respective operating theatres.

CHAPTER 37

CLARE

THE FIRST THING I'm aware of is a beeping sound. A disembodied voice floats in from somewhere and tells me that I am on the recovery ward. My eyelids feel too heavy to lift open. I am terribly thirsty. I try and say *water* and hope somebody understands. Presently I feel myself being lifted up, the oxygen mask over my nose and mouth is raised, and a straw is placed in my mouth. The disembodied voice tells me to take a few sips but no more than that. The water must be some sort of nectar for the gods, so wonderful does it taste.

I flop back down against the pillows as the oxygen mask is replaced. The same voice tells me I have been given morphine and that I have a catheter inserted. I come to the conclusion that I don't really care about anything. The hospital could burn down around me and I would not be concerned. I am safely enveloped in the arms of Morpheus. I am agreeably and most comfortably numb.

However, as the reversing agent goes about its job, very

soon I am slightly more with it and am told I can be taken back to the ward. I am aware that the bed has started to move, and I force my eyes open. As soon as the recovery room doors open I can see James looking at me, and I smile at him weakly.

"Hello darling." He stoops over the bed briefly. "I've been waiting for you to come out."

The oxygen mask is in the way of any meaningful conversation. Ross hovers in the background. When I see him I suddenly wonder about Izzy, but can't really articulate what I want to say.

I can see that James and Ross are following me back to our room. I am surrounded by monitors, drips and tubes. I feel a twinge of pain down in the lower abdomen.

"Click on the morphine pump if you feel any pain." The nurse checks my cannula. "Don't worry; you can't overdose. It will only give you a certain amount every hour."

James holds my hand, and Ross disappears out of the room presumably to give us privacy or to go back and wait for Izzy. I close my eyes, and listen to my husband's voice.

"Izzy is still in surgery. As far as we know, the operation is going well."

I close my eyes and drift away.

As consciousness creeps up on me again I can hear a low rumble of male voices. This time my eyes are a little easier to open, and I take in the sight of Izzy asleep in the bed next to me surrounded by tubes, bags and monitors. At the foot of our beds sit James and Ross, both now smiling over at me as I struggle to sit up.

"Take it easy." James jumps up from his chair. "Would

you like a sip of water?"

I nod furiously, and wince at stabs of pain shooting around my lower regions.

"Yes please." I whisper.

Once again the water tastes like manna from heaven. I wonder why I don't feel the need to pee, but then realise as I wake up a bit more that I have a catheter inserted. I feel embarrassed that Ross must be able to see all my urine draining into a bag. If he can see it he takes no notice; instead he smiles over at me and gives me a quick reminder.

"Don't forget your morphine drip if you have any pain." I had forgotten all about that. I turn my head to the left, and there is my saviour; a drip stand, a full cylinder of morphine, and an on/off button just waiting to be clicked.

I press the button, allowing morphine to run in through the cannula.

The pain recedes, and I lever myself up in the bed. James plonks himself down on the side of my bed.

"How do you feel?"

"Dazed."

"You will do for quite a while. That liquid cosh is good stuff."

"You're telling me. I don't even remember going to sleep. Any sign of life from Izzy?" I glance over to my right.

"Not yet, she's still out cold."

"Just think about what sort of house you're going to buy." Ross yawns in his chair. "That should make you feel a bit better."

I had forgotten all about that as well. My brain is AWOL. The sudden thought that two million pounds will soon be making its way to my bank account causes me to smile at Ross."

"It certainly helps, yes." I chuckle and lay back down. "I feel guilty taking so much money from you."

"Don't." Ross shakes his head. "It's all yours."

When I awake again and look around the room I can see both James and Ross have nodded off in the two armchairs, and that Izzy is still asleep.

I grab the time to feast my eyes undisturbed on Ross's features. The years have been kind to him; the blond hair is only just beginning to show wisps of silver, and despite the years of touring debauchery his face has only the usual laughter lines around his mouth and the inevitable crows' feet which affects us all. His body is a little more solid than I remember, and my mind suddenly darts back to a vision of a young, suntanned Adonis wearing frayed Levi shorts and not much else. Despite my resolution to forget the past, my heart still aches with love for a man that will never be mine.

Beside me my sister stirs, and as though he is tuned in to her every want and need, Ross wakes up and walks over to her bed. I close my eyes as I hear him whispering softly and helping her to take a sip of water. A nurse coming in wakes James, who smiles at me from the other side of the room.

"You're doing great Clare."

I return his smile with one of my own. I feel incredibly hungry. When the nurse has completed her observations and bustles off to make me some toast, I take my mind off my hunger and try to figure out how many loaves of bread two million pounds could buy.

CHAPTER 38

IZZY

THE DIGITAL CLOCK on one of my monitors reads 02:16. I wake up again but have no idea what day it is or how long I have been asleep. I have an oxygen mask over my face, and I seem to be connected to a heart monitor and drips of some sort. I can feel a catheter is in place.

I take off the oxygen mask and lever myself up. The faint aroma of toast lingers in the air, and I have a sudden yearning for thick, runny cheddar cheese melted onto a huge doorstep slice of white buttery toast. I should be so lucky.

I glance over to my left. Clare is asleep. Ross and James have gone, and there are just two armchairs facing each other across a coffee table where they sat. Despite Clare being next to me I feel very much alone, and I have a sudden need to be in Ross's arms and for him to tell me everything is going to be alright.

In the still of the night my mind tries to focus on everything the renal nurse relayed to me; *was it yesterday?* Take temperature and blood pressure for signs of rejection. Don't lift anything. Watch out for ureteral leak, wound infection, stomach ulcers and brittle bones. Don't forget the skin cancer; wear sun-cream. Keep your hand on your ha'penny for three weeks. Keep taking the fucking tablets every day, all fifteen of them. I'm not sure if my confused brain has forgotten anything.

Nurse Never-Seems-to-Laugh comes in and takes more readings. She grunts with satisfaction and I ask her if I can eat anything. She shakes her head and points to a glucose drip going into my cannula. I catch her drift that apparently later on today I will be able to eat something light. I can't wait.

The nurse checks Clare's monitors, and replaces one of the drips. There's a beeping noise as she sets up a new bag, and Clare wakes up. At least I've got some company now.

"Hi." I smile at my sister and take off my oxygen mask as soon as the nurse goes away. "How's it going?"

"I don't know." Clare yawns. "What day is it?"

"God knows." I shrug. "Have you eaten some toast?"

"Guilty." Clare pulls a face. "Sorry."

"It's alright for you; all I get are pills. It's tablet city here; fifteen of the buggers to take every morning until I croak."

I notice that I've made Clare smile at last.   It feels good. She sits up and looks at me.

"You're definitely on the pill then…....."

"Not *that* one." I make a face. "I like the bit about having to wait at least three weeks for a bit of the other as well. I can't remember the last time I felt energetic enough to stay awake in bed for anything other than sleep anyway."

"James will have to tie a knot in it as well for a while." Clare grins. "At least I've got a good excuse now."

"You need an excuse?" I roll my eyes heavenwards. "After feeling like death for years I've got a list of them as long as your arm."

"Go on then." My sister laughs, but then clutches her abdomen. "No, you'd better not; it hurts too much."

"Headache, earache, fanny ache, leg ache, brain ache….."

"Fanny ache?" Clare laughs and then presses the morphine pump.

"Yeah, that's the best one. A burning fanny, that's even better."

Clare grins and lays back down on the pillows.

"I'll have to give that one a go."

It's 07:45 and the boys are back, but we send them out again because we want to look our best. It's all about keeping up appearances even though you feel like *shit*. We've managed to ditch the oxygen masks, but I still have the heart monitor on. However, nothing looks as inviting as a bowl of hot water and a bar of soap and a flannel when you're stuck in bed.

I reach for a comb on my bedside cabinet. My hair is so thin and brittle; I'm sure I'm going bald. I don't want to look in a mirror, and so just comb it the way I've always done. Clare rummages around in her make-up bag for a brush. I'm taken back to the days before I had ever heard of kidney disease.

"Remember when Mum used to complain that our hair was always blocking up the shower? Mine was down to my waist and yours wasn't much shorter."

"Yes; Dad always got the job of emptying the filter." Clare nods. "I used to blame it on you."

"And I on you." I sigh. "I still miss them sometimes, you know."

Clare turns to look at me as she brushes her hair.

"Me too; or is it because they were Mum and Dad and we knew we were protected against *anything*?"

"Possibly. Somehow when Rachel came along it just wasn't the same."

"No, you're right." Clare nods in agreement. "I never really got on with her."

"The wicked stepmother. I couldn't believe she kept all Dad's money for herself."

"She certainly did." Clare put on some lip gloss. "I never saw a penny of it."

"I'm sorry." I say with genuine sympathy. "You really got a shit deal, didn't you?"

Clare looks at me in surprise.

"I've got a good husband and two lovely children. What more could I need?"

The words lie unspoken between us. I know that because of me she has missed out on the husband she wanted and the kind of lifestyle that the ordinary person in the street could only dream about. To assuage my guilt I encouraged Ross to give her a taste of that lifestyle, but in reality the money has probably arrived thirty years too late.

CHAPTER 39

JAMES

THANK GOODNESS CLARE'S recovering well and can leave hospital tomorrow, but she will need to go back again in a few days for a follow up. I've been given my marching orders back to Gatwick; my wife now wants me to go home and pay the cheque in. Ross has been the perfect host and without a doubt is the most generous man I've ever met, but I still don't like the thought of her staying at his house for another week. Izzy still has to remain at the hospital; the kidney isn't producing any urine yet, and so in the evenings there'll be just the two of them there. With their past relationship I feel very uneasy, but there's Matty to look after and I can't impose on Lauren's good nature any longer.

Ross wrote a letter for me to show any bank staff raising their eyebrows at the sight of a cheque for two million pounds. I take the cheque out of my wallet when I'm alone and gaze at it. It doesn't seem real at the moment; perhaps when the money actually shows up in our account then I'll believe I'm a millionaire. At the moment it's just like Monopoly money.

He doesn't say much to me when we return from the hospital each evening, because he has to spend most of the time in his study on the phone. He has another life which brings in the money that we're not part of, and to be quite honest I feel as if I'm in the way. I don't want him to think that he has to entertain me, and so as soon as I get back to the house I usually go straight to the guest room after we've had dinner. His phone starts ringing even while we're eating, and sometimes he takes his meal into the study. I know that once he starts talking on the phone I'll probably not see him again for the rest of the night, but to be honest I think both of us are happier that way. Is he like that with Clare? He's not unfriendly, but we're two strangers really, and our lives are worlds apart. We meet up for breakfast, and he's usually chatty enough, but after a while we run out of things to say and are grateful to be able to set off and see the girls.

Clare's sitting in the armchair and fully dressed when we get there. Izzy is still in bed and hooked up to her drips. We give Ross and Izzy some privacy and walk down to the day room. Clare is still in a little pain and is feeling weak and tired, but I'm glad to see she's on her feet. The day room is empty, and I steal a quick kiss.

"How are you feeling today?"

"Much better; they're obsessed with my bladder and bowels though."

"Well they would be." I chuckle and follow her over to a seat. "I wouldn't expect otherwise."

"It would just be nice to be able to pee without someone wanting to see it."

I hide a grin.

"How's the pain?"

"Still there; they'll give me some painkillers to take home. Other than that I'm okay, but not allowed to lift anything for six weeks. Hopefully I'll be allowed to go back with you and Ross later."

"Can I see your scar?"

"Bugger off."

My wife is on the road to recovery I can tell. Now all we have to do is to spend two million pounds. She smiles at me as if she knows what I'm thinking.

"You haven't lost that cheque, have you?"

"As if! I'm guarding it with my life!" I grin back at her.

"Have you heard from Lauren and Matty? We're not allowed to use mobiles in here."

"They sent texts asking how you were. I haven't told them about the money yet. I just said you were getting on okay."

"No, we'll have to break it to them gently." Clare looks thoughtful for a moment. "We're on the verge of a new life James. It's exciting."

"Yes." I nodded. "I still can't believe it though." "Ross won't let us down."

How does she know? Is my wife of 30 plus years going on past experience? If truth be told he seems to have let her down rather badly in 1970. What if it's all a lie and the cheque bounces? Nobody can gain access to his house if he doesn't want them there. Has this all been a set-up just to keep his wife alive? Has Clare been taken in by him yet again?

I'm aware that Clare is looking at me. She reaches over and takes my hand.

"Penny for your thoughts."

I sigh and stroke her fingers.

"Is he for real?   I mean…..who the hell gives someone two million pounds?"

"*He* does." Clare answers in a soft voice. "Go home, pay the cheque in, and you'll see."

"So you want to get rid of me then?"

"No; I just want you to realise that he means what he says."

"Do you love him?" I search her face and carry on stroking her fingers.

"I did once, but not anymore. I've grown up, James. It's taken God knows how long, but I now see him for what he is."

"And what's that?"

"My brother-in-law; my sister's husband."

The flight home hits a little turbulence, and I'm on edge as the landing gear engages. I applaud the pilot along with all the other passengers as the plane lands safely, and hurry to the baggage collection point. If I can get around the M25 and onto the M11 before the rush hour starts I can make the bank in time for closing.

I wait impatiently for the courtesy bus, and am the first one to jump on when it arrives. It's still raining; in fact it probably hasn't stopped since I've been gone. I look out the window of the bus as it rattles along to the car park; nobody going about their daily business at the airport knows I'm holding on to a cheque for two million pounds. I feel in my back pocket to make sure my wallet is still there, and give it a comforting pat.

I get to the bank with an hour to spare. There's no way I'm going to queue at the counter and let everybody hear the ensuing conversation, so I ask a young member of staff standing around like a spare prick at a wedding if I can see one of the managers privately. The chap ushers me into an empty booth, and goes off to find the next in command. Presently I am joined by an older man in a pinstripe suit and glasses, who regards me inquisitively.

"I am Peter East, Assistant Manager. How can I help you?"

"I'd like to pay this in please, but obviously with as little fanfare as possible."

I open my wallet and give him the cheque. In true British style he does a very good impression of somebody not at all impressed.

"Very well, Sir, but it will take five working days to clear."

"Of course. I have my bank card here so that you can access my account."

"I will pay it in now for you, and bring you a receipt."

"Thanks very much. Please could you send me an updated statement?"

"Yes we can do that for a small charge."

"That will be great, thanks."

I check the post every day. Halfway through the following week I receive a bank statement, and open the envelope with a racing heart. The total amount in our current account excluding the odd change is two million, three thousand and seventy four pounds. We are millionaires.

CHAPTER 40

CLARE

I AM SENDING a telepathic message to my kidney, as it stubbornly refuses to work in Izzy's body. It's my last day in France today. After I've had my follow up appointment at the hospital and said goodbye to Izzy I will go back with Ross to their house for another night, and then he will drive me to Laroche airport tomorrow morning. He's organised VIP treatment for me; I won't have to lift any bags at all. I'll feel just like a rock star as I step onto the plane. Although I can still feel the pull of the stitched wound, I feel less tired and more able to travel now, and can't wait to get home. James has just sent me a text to let me know that the money is in our account. I'm still coming to terms with the reality of our new situation.

With one hand supporting my lower abdomen I walk slowly down the grand staircase to the breakfast room. I can hear Ross in the study talking on the phone. I think he wants to re-schedule the upcoming tour, and obviously that will make more work for Paul. I have a nasty feeling that the tickets have already been printed.

Marie has left a selection of hot plates, and I help myself to scrambled eggs, toast and coffee. Ross joins me as I bite into a second piece of toast.

"Sorry about the phone calls." Ross sits down opposite me and pours himself some coffee. "I want to keep an eye on Izzy now. She's getting depressed at the thought of lifetime dialysis. I've made Paul's day and told him I'm thinking of postponing the tour. "

"It's a little soon to worry yet, isn't it?" I venture. "I thought the doctor said it could take up to six weeks?"

"I know, but if the kidney's still not working at the end of six weeks I'll need to be around for the fallout. I can't be off traipsing all around the world with the band."

"Give it a little more time." I smile at him. "I've had a word with my kidney and encouraged it to buck its ideas up."

"What did you say to it?" Ross chuckles.

"I told it to stop pissing about." I grin at him.

"*Stop* pissing about? We *want* it to piss about as much as it can!"

I laugh at the pun through a mouthful of egg, and then look up at him. He reaches an arm over the table and places his hand on top of mine.

"Dear Clare, you're a real tonic. Izzy and I have so much to thank you for."

I shake my head, but keep my hand under his.

"It's the other way around. You've made us richer than we ever imagined. You'll be the first ones through the door of our new house."

"It's the least I could do." Ross retracts his arm. "I fucked up your life and it's payback time."

"No, don't ever think that." I look up. "I've got no complaints."

"I want to apologise here and now. I was a total prat."

I do not really want to be reminded of that time. It was too long ago, and all I want to do now is forget about it.

"You fell in love with your soul mate. Let's move on. I want to see Izzy today before I go home."

"And you shall." Ross nodded. "I'll drop you off at the hospital and leave the two of you for an hour or so; I need to come back here and do some organising."

"Don't cancel the tour yet; give it another couple of weeks." I finish my breakfast and stand up. "I'm sure things will work out."

"We shall see." Ross shrugs and drains his cup.

My sister smiles at me as I pop my head around the door. My bed has been removed, and the room seems so much bigger.

"Come in!" She sits up in bed. "I've been so looking forward to seeing you."

"Last day today." I sit in the visitor's armchair. "I'm off home tomorrow."

Izzy still looks tired and drained, but for some reason she cannot stop smiling.

"I've had some good news this morning."

"What?" I catch on to her good mood and grin back at her.

"My creatinine level is coming down. It looks as though the kidney might be starting to work."

"Oh! That's wonderful!" I jump up as quickly as I'm able to and give her a hug. "Have you told Ross?"

"Not yet." Izzy shakes her head. "I wanted you to be

the first one to know.”

“We ought to have a little celebration.” I chuckle.

“If I was allowed to drink champagne I’d open up a bottle or twelve.” Izzy sighed and settled herself more comfortably. “Having you back in my life is the best thing; the kidney comes in a close second though.” She gave me an impish smile.

“What about me?” I grin. “I’ve got two million pounds, and it’s all due to *you*!”

“Don’t spend it all at once.” Izzy waggles a forefinger at me as her features take on a more serious look. “It’s to compensate for the life you missed out on. You must think about it sometimes.”

“I used to; not anymore. I’ve realised that you can’t make somebody love you. You have to move on. I found a decent man who thinks I’m the best thing since sliced bread. I can’t ask for any more than that.”

“You can’t indeed.” Izzy agreed. “James is a good chap; much better than the long haired layabout from the Art College you brought home that time.”

I smile as I remember a long-ago evening.

“Do you remember Dad’s face when he saw Ross? It was a picture, wasn’t it?”

“I didn’t notice. I was too busy looking at Ross. I’d never seen anything so beautiful. I knew right then and there that he was the one for me.” Izzy sighed. “It was terrible.”

“He obviously thought the same.” I reach across the bed and hold her hand. “Don’t fret over things that can’t be changed.”

“We must never lose touch again.” Izzy squeezes my fingers. “You and James are welcome to come and stay anytime. I want to get to know Lauren and Matty too. After all, I'm their auntie."

"And Rachel tells me you have a whole brood of grandchildren running about. Have you got some photos?"

"Have I ever!"

By the time Ross returns I have learned the names of their five grandchildren and can recognise their features from a concertina-like album of photos that Izzy carries in her bag. I pick up on their fondness for little Solenn. I realise with some sadness that all five children know nothing of me or James at all, and would probably walk right past us if they saw us in the street.

I go to make a graceful exit as soon as I see Ross, but they both shake their heads.

"You're staying right here." Izzy points back to my chair. "We've got some news for Ross, don't forget."

"Oh?" Ross kisses Izzy and plumps himself down on the side of her bed. "What?"

"Creatinine levels are decreasing."

I was unprepared for Ross's dramatic reaction to Izzy's almost matter-of-fact statement. His eyes filled with tears and he covered his face with his hands.

"Oh God!" He sobbed.

I saw Izzy stroke his arm and wanted to be three thousand miles away.

"Don't upset yourself." Izzy murmured.

"It's great news darling, but I should have listened to Clare all along."

I pricked up my ears at the mention of my name.

"What d'you mean?" Izzy looked at me and I shrugged.

Ross wiped his eyes and exhaled with force.

"I've just gone and cancelled the whole fucking tour!"

CHAPTER 41

ROSS

MY IZZY WILL live! After Clare and I returned to the house she sent me a text to say the kidney had actually produced a few drops of urine. Who would have ever thought I'd want to howl at the moon with joy at hearing the news that my wife has been able to piss?

It's Clare's last evening, and so I don't feel as though I should spend it all on the phone talking to my son. Paul's going in to see Izzy tonight, and thank God he says it's not too late to reinstate the tour. He'd not got around to breaking the news to the band anyway, and so I'm still in their good books. Darryl and Chaz would have spent all their money by now and will need to make some more. I don't know how my brother can get through so much dough in such a short space of time; I think that wife of his has something to do with it. Chaz is just a fucking alcoholic.

Sometimes the pressure of being the main songwriter and carrying Darryl and the others is overwhelming. I've tried to stay off the weed as much as I can; Izzy hates it when I smoke a joint. I've found something much better actually, but as yet she hasn't found out just what it is. Rudy found me on the last tour; a thousand Rudys have tried getting to me before, but I wasn't in my fifties then. I'm actually losing interest in touring; I haven't got the energy for it anymore. As I become older I prefer to stay at home with Izzy and the family. I'm not an addict or anywhere near being addicted, but there's no getting away from it; chasing the dragon is definitely hitting the right spot just now. I can deal with the pressures of touring and with Izzy's illness, scribble down some songs, sort out the band's arguments, and even be pleasant to Clare and forget 30 years of arse-ache. I'm careful; I haven't got a death wish or anything like that. It's for recreation only; it keeps me sane and helps me wind down. I can stop it any time I like.

Clare seems quiet; she's gone upstairs to start packing. I'm not sure if I ought to do something special for her last night. I assume she's still in a bit of pain, although she doesn't complain much. I'll ask Marie to cook us something nice; maybe some steaks or venison.

My phone beeps; it's Rudy. Rudy knows by some sort of second sight when I'm getting low. He's at the gate and says he has some really good gear this time. I can nip out to Rudy, get the stuff and chill out while Clare's packing and getting ready for dinner. She'll never know I'm high as a kite; I'm good at keeping it all together. Marcel will wonder why I'm not letting Rudy in again, but I'll just say I don't want him in the house. Well, I don't actually; he's just my man and I don't want to be friends with the fucker.

Marcel's at the door, but I tell him to find Marie and let her know to cook some nice steaks for us. While he's gone I run down the drive and open the gate for Rudy, who warns me the smack's purer than usual. I nod and give him a wad of notes and a little extra for his trouble.

Does Marcel know what's going on? Who knows? He's his usual discreet self as I run back to the house. I have a feeling he *does* know somehow. Rudy's been coming here for quite a few months now since Izzy's been ill. I'll have to stop him driving up to the house when Izzy's back on her feet. She's a smart cookie; there's no fooling her. When she's well she's on the ball; she'll sniff out Rudy in no time. Don't get me wrong; I'm going to stop when Izzy's home and well again, but maybe I'll need some stuff before I go on tour.

I smell of hospitals and illness. The house is quiet; Clare is probably having a nap. It feels good to step into the shower and wash off the day's dirt and grime. Izzy's news has put me in a good mood, and the smack will put me in an even better one. I'll be able to face Clare tonight. I know she still has the hots for me; I can sense it every time I'm near her. It was never Clare; just Izzy. It might have been for a brief moment when I first met her, but that's many years in the past. I expect Clare will be more emotional than usual at dinner; I hope to God she doesn't come on to me. I'll have to tell her once and for all that I just don't find her attractive. It was only ever Izzy, and it still is for me.

I can't even be bothered to get dressed; my anticipation for the rush of smack is greater. I've become quite the chemist in my spare time; I can cook up a feast in a syringe. It's even better than the fillet steak and chips Marie will concoct in about two hours' time.

I lie back on the bed and tie the tourniquet. I think back to the first time I met Izzy; the dark hair, the smouldering looks, and the flashing midnight blue eyes. I was smitten straight away; how could a bloke not be with such a hot chick? Sometimes I still can't believe that she gave up her career for a waster like me. That's what I am, a waster; one of life's tossers. Donald was right back in 1970; he had me sized up in no time.

As I push the plunger and a shot of liquid gold enters my veins, I drift away on a cloud of Izzy. I don't even care that I've forgotten to set my alarm for dinner……..

CHAPTER 42

CLARE

I'M ALL PACKED, showered, and ready for dinner. I'm quite hungry actually. My appetite has come back and I think I'm finally over the liquid cosh at last. Anaesthetics are strange; you think you'd sleep for a week afterwards, but actually for the first three days after the operation every time I drifted off to sleep I would wake up again with a start. It must be something to do with the drugs they give you to bring you round. What I definitely *do* know is that they all mess with your brain something terrible. I've managed a nap this afternoon, and I feel quite like my old self now.

I can't hear any voices downstairs, but I'll go and hang around in the dining room. It's nearly eight o'clock, so dinner must be ready. I hope Ross likes my dress. I feel I have to make an effort for my last night here, but then again I don't suppose for a minute that he'll take much notice of what I'm wearing anyway.

A delicious aroma hits me as I walk downstairs; it smells

like steak and onions, and maybe even chips. My mouth begins to water. It occurs to me that if James and I manage the money properly we may even be able to hire a cook. To not have to think about what to prepare for dinner every night is a luxury only a few can afford. I must thank Ross again this evening; he's changed our lives in ways he will never realise.

The table is set and the wine is chilling nicely in the ice bucket. Ross is nowhere to be seen. I wave to Marie as she pops her head around the dining room door.

"Where is M'sieu Tyler?" Marie checks the dining room as she speaks. "Dinner is ready."

"I'll have a look for him; he's probably on the phone in his study."

I feel a little disappointed that Ross cannot be bothered to arrive for dinner on time. As I walk out into the foyer towards the study, the grandfather clock chimes the hour. I arrive at the study, but it is firmly locked. I knock, but realise after a few minutes that nobody is inside. I check the main lounge, which is also empty.

Hunger forces me straight back upstairs to Ross and Izzy's bedroom, and I knock lightly on the door.

"Ross, it's Clare! Dinner's ready!"

There is no answer. It occurs to me that he might have taken a nap, and so I open the door quietly so as not to startle him. The room is in darkness, and I fish about on the wall for the light switch. I can feel three dimmer switches close together just inside the door on the right, and turn the first dimmer around which lights up half of the bedroom.

The room is vast, with wall-to-wall wardrobes and

cabinets. The same white shag pile carpet as in the guest room covers the floor. The bed is in darkness through an archway, and I fiddle with the right hand dimmer switch. Immediately spotlights shine down upon the bed, and I can see that Ross is asleep.

However, as I walk nearer to the bed my heart begins to beat faster in my chest, because I am frightened at the sight which greets me. Ross lies naked on his back upon the bed, very pale, almost yellow in colour. His chest is still; he looks dead. On one arm there is a tourniquet tied, and a syringe embedded in the fold of skin on the inside of his elbow. A medium-sized tin on his bedside table contains all the equipment I think a drug addict would need in order to satisfy his craving.

I try to scream, but no sound comes out. My bowels turn to water and I have to run to his en-suite to relieve myself. Horrified, I step back into the bedroom. I go up to him and put an ear to his chest. His body is stone cold, and there is no heartbeat. I put my right fist on top of my left hand and press down on his chest for five beats and then breathe into his mouth. I carry on with this like an automaton in desperation for ten minutes, but there is no response.

The love of my life has gone, just like a leaf in an autumn breeze. Sobbing uncontrollably I listen to his chest again, but if truth be told I realise he must have died a couple of hours ago. I was singing unconcerned in the shower whilst Ross was shooting his veins full of poison.

My tears fall on his face as I kiss his cold forehead and tell him that I love him, that I have always loved him, and that I will love him until my own dying breath. I cover him with a blanket. Nobody must see him naked; there is no dignity in it. I leave the tourniquet and syringe where it is and straighten his hair. There is nothing more I can do.

Downstairs I can hear Marie calling us to dinner. I suddenly cannot eat a thing. I must go and break the news and phone James. Police and medics will soon be swarming all over the house like flies as the steaks grow cold and the wine remains untouched. As I compose myself and walk shakily down the stairs it suddenly occurs to me that Izzy does not know. I will need to tell Marcel so that he can drive me to the hospital. My sister needs me, more than she has ever needed me before. I must go to her as soon as I can get away.

The nurse in charge gives me a black look as I walk into the ward at half past ten that night, after giving a statement to the police. I am past caring what she thinks.

"I have to see Madame Tyler. I'm afraid I have very bad news for her, which will not wait."

"Very well, but try not to stay too long. Madame needs her rest."

Izzy is asleep as I quietly enter the room. I hate to wake her, knowing that the recent moments of happiness we have shared will be all she has to cling to in the days and weeks to come.

"Izzy; it's Clare."

My sister is awake. One look at my face tells her the situation is bad.

"What is it?" She looks past me towards the door. "Where's Ross?"

It's as if she knows something is wrong already. I instinctively hug her and am in tears again before I can even utter a word.

"I don't know how to tell you this." I sob.

"Has something happened to Ross?" Izzy leans against me with a long sigh.

How can I bring myself to tell her the truth? However, it must be done. I steel myself.

"He's dead, Izzy. I'm so sorry. I found him on his bed this evening; it looks to me like some sort of drug overdose. The doctor confirmed death tonight at nine o'clock."

My sister collapses against me and I hold her frail body close as, desolate and beside herself with grief, she mourns the death of her soul mate. We cry together, both unable to imagine life without him.

"I want to see him!" Izzy wails. "I won't believe he's dead until I see him!"

"He's been brought here to this mortuary until a funeral director is appointed." My tears fall into her hair. "I'll go there with you tomorrow."

The night is just beginning; the longest night of our lives.

CHAPTER 43

IZZY

CLARE HAS BEEN my rock throughout the night. I don't know what I would have done without her. We've just sat here hugging each other until dawn began to break. I've just phoned Daisy and Paul to break the news; my poor babies are grief-stricken. Clare told the police not to phone them.

I still can't believe it has happened. I know Ross had an addictive personality, but was unaware of the depths of his dependency on drugs. I've been so ill that I've taken my eye off the ball. If only I had been well enough I'm sure his drug habit would not have passed me by. I hold myself partly responsible for his death, although Clare tells me there is no way it's my fault. She says the only person who could have stopped Ross was Ross himself, but loving him so much as I do, I *know* I could have helped him.

Paul and Daisy are on their way; the three of us will go to the mortuary viewing room together. I need to spare my sister the horror of it; she's done so much already. She seemed greatly relieved when I told her that she doesn't need to come with me. She's already seen him lifeless, and she is on her knees with tiredness. Marcel has driven her back to the house to rest. She's missed her plane, but says she will stay here with me at least until after the autopsy and funeral. I can't possibly think about his body being cut about and then buried. The whole scenario is unreal.

There are no words to say when my children arrive. They sit either side of me on the bed and we hug each other. Our grief is so raw, I cannot imagine the pain ever going away. Ross was here with me only hours ago, and now he lies dead on a mortuary slab. I can't seem to get my head around it. Is life really that precarious? One minute you're here and then gone the next?

A member of staff from the general office appears in my room and introduces herself as Pascale. She wears a black skirt and jacket and a white blouse. I hate black, and think I will detest the colour for the rest of my life. The three of us stand up, although I feel as though my legs are going to collapse. Paul brings me a wheelchair, and we follow Pascale out of the ward towards the direction of the mortuary.

It is about a five minute walk through the maze of interconnecting corridors until we arrive at the viewing room. I have never seen a dead body, let alone my husband's. I hope to God it's not Ross; maybe somebody has died who looks like him. I'm frightened I might vomit. I swallow and feel glad that I am sitting down.

There is a corridor down by the side of the mortuary, with a door leading off to the right. Pascale unlocks the door and tactfully retreats. We enter a small room where to my horror Ross is laid out in a coffin. My eyes become fixated on his face, which is a sort of waxy saffron colour. His eyes are closed, and his lifeless hands are resting on a white padded counterpane. Behind me I can hear Daisy crying. I reach up and Paul holds my hand. None of us know what to do or say.

The feeling of nausea passes as I look at my husband remembering all the good times we had shared over nearly 30 years of being together. I ask Paul to push me nearer to the coffin, and I take hold of one of Ross's hands. I am not frightened anymore of his dead body. He never hurt me in life, and he certainly won't be hurting me in death. He is still wearing his wedding ring. It doesn't feel like the hand I used to hold at all, which had always been there to comfort and embrace me and to make everything right. I have to come to terms with the fact that everything will never be right again. He has left me all the money I will ever need, but he is gone. The body in front of me is just a shell.

I tell him I love him, then take his wedding ring off and place it on my thumb, the only one of my digits it will fit on without falling off. I kiss his fingers, and let go of his hand. I have seen enough; the three of us are physical wrecks. Daisy kisses his forehead, but Paul just stands behind me stoically.

I indicate towards the door, and Paul pushes the wheelchair. Outside Pascale waits patiently. She gives me a thin smile as we exit, and then locks the door. I show her Ross's wedding ring which I have taken. She nods and says she will make a note of it.

When I get back to my room I twist Ross's ring around and around on my finger. He had never taken it off in all the years we had been married. I am a widow now. I will never see my husband again. All I have left of him is a wedding ring. I bury my face in Paul's shoulder and sob.

The autopsy results are splattered all over the newspapers; death by heroin overdose. My husband becomes one of those statistics you read about in well-thumbed magazines found in dentists' and doctors' surgeries. By the time I am allowed home Paul and Daisy have arranged the funeral between them. Because of who he is it will be quite a lavish affair. We will be bringing him home to England, to his hometown of Portsmouth, to be buried in the family plot. The service will be in Portsmouth cathedral in three days' time. I do not want to go, but I know I must. I am still feeling weak, but Clare tells me she will stay with me for as long as I need her to. Her kidney pulses in my body, and it is as though we are one person, with all hatred and bitterness between us forgotten. This terrible event has brought us even closer together. There is a bond between us that nothing and nobody will ever break. In the midst of life we are in death, so they say. Clare gave me life to cope with Ross's death. I must carry on for her sake, even though in my blackest moments I sometimes feel like joining my husband.

CHAPTER 44

JAMES

IT SEEMS I am invited to the funeral. Clare phoned to tell me apparently 500 mourners will attend. I didn't even know the bloke very well, even though he was my brother-in-law, but he gave me two million pounds so it's the least I can do to hotfoot it down to Portsmouth and help give him a good send-off. Clare and Izzy will be flying back later on today, with Paul, Daisy, their partners, and the coffin. The Press and fans have got wind of it; there's going to be a quiet riot at Stanstead I expect. Apparently they'll all be staying at The Best Western Hotel, not far from the cathedral. The undertakers are meeting them at Stanstead, and will then drive Clare home first. It will be good to see her again.

There's an unopened suitcase in the hall when Matty and I return from school. Clare sits pale and tired-looking on the sofa, holding a cup of coffee. I run towards her and put my arms around her. Matty holds back for a moment.

"It's good to have you back." I kiss her and make room for Matty, who sits down beside her. "Somebody else here wants to say hello."

"Hi Mum." Matty kisses Clare and looks pleased to have her back. "Do you feel okay?"

"I'm alright." Clare smiles at him and gives him a hug. "I'm just a bit tired, that's all."

"Lauren is cooking tonight; you don't have to do a thing. She'll be home soon." I want to help her as much as I can.

My wife makes no move to get off the sofa. I'm not sure if it's the after-effects of the operation or Ross's death, but she appears somehow defeated. She holds her coffee with both hands and stares ahead. I venture a question.

"What was it like at the airport?"

She brings the cup to her lips and takes a small sip.

"Pandemonium; Press everywhere. We were expecting a dignified transfer of the coffin to the hearse. No such luck; flashbulbs popping, photographers on ladders, fans crowding behind the barriers. It was a bloody carnival."

"Did you expect it any other way?" I look at her, surprised.

"I thought the Press might have given us some privacy, but no; poor old Ross still makes the front page even when he's lying in his coffin." She wiped away a tear. "It's Izzy I feel sorry for as well; she's not really recovered and she has to go through all this."

"She's strong; she'll get through it."

Clare perks up a bit when Lauren's key turns in the door. She stands up and goes out to greet her. I smile to see Lauren hold out her arms to Clare.

"Mum! I'm so glad you're home again!"

Clare is tearful at the sight of Lauren. I watch them hugging and crying, and have a pang of regret that Matty and I cannot be as free and unbridled with our emotions as my two girls obviously are.

It's about a three hour trip down to Portsmouth. The day of the funeral dawns bright and clear, and Clare is up before the alarm. Izzy has told us not to wear black. It feels strange going to a funeral in light colours, but that's the way she wants it. Clare dresses in a pink and white checked suit; she looks gorgeous, and my heart aches with love for her. When this is all over I can't wait to buy the sort of house that Ross wanted for us; perhaps it will put a smile back on her face. Lauren and Matty want to meet their aunt and cousins, and have decided to attend too. The house is a hive of activity by 07:30.

Clare doesn't speak much as I drive down the A3. Lauren and Matty chatter quietly in the back, full of expectation; unwilling to let on to Clare how excited they are at the thought of seeing faces they only usually look at on television. Matty has already asked me if he can take photos of celebrities in the cathedral and sell them to the newspapers. I silently applaud my son's entrepreneurial skills, but tell him, alas, no.

The nave organ is playing quietly, as we enter through the cathedral's bronze West doors. I notice the coffin standing on a plinth by the altar, covered in lilies and white carnations. Clare is to sit with Izzy at the front, and walks nervously down to join her sister. I don't mind the fact that the kids and I are relegated to the back pews; we can get a better view of the famous faces from our perch in the cheap seats. I can hear Lauren gasping every five minutes as another celebrity arrives. I give her a nudge and tell her to shut up.

Not being religious I don't take too much notice of the service. I'm more concerned with looking around the cathedral and seeing if there are any faces that I recognise. There are plenty, and I can almost hear Matty's brain whirring as he makes a mental list of the congregation to regurgitate the next day at school.

Clare and her sister sit close together. As individual celebrities step up to the dais and give their tributes, I can see that both Izzy and Clare are visibly shaking with grief. It disturbs me somehow that my wife is so upset at Ross's passing. Has she carried a torch for him all these years? Am I still only second best? Indeed, have I been just second best for the entire length of our marriage? It is a sobering thought, and one on which I do not care to linger.

When the service and hymns are over the celebrities disappear like the puff of smoke they are, leaving us to a private burial in the Tyler plot in Kingston cemetery. Clare goes to the cemetery with Izzy and the immediate family in the front limousine, and I follow behind in our car along with members of Ross's family. As we stand around the open grave Izzy and Clare clutch each other and weep. I feel uncomfortable at my wife's show of grief; it's as though she has forgotten that her husband and children are there, relegated once again to the back row. I try and catch her eye at one point, but she looks right through me. I am sad and dismayed not to be in a position to offer any comfort to her at all.

CHAPTER 45

CLARE

SO MUCH ANGUISH and sadness, and the finality of the burial; I feel broken in two. To have loved somebody for so long and then to have them taken away forever is utterly heart-rending. I am now a wealthy woman, but would give it all back to Ross if only he could return to us. I know he loved only Izzy, but the knowledge that he was alive and back in our lives albeit at a distance was enough to keep me going through any bad times. Now there is a black hole that only his huge personality can fill; I don't know how I will be able to return to Izzy's house in the future knowing that Ross will not be there.

James is trying his best to cheer me up. He wants us to go house-hunting, and I suppose it will be good for me to go along with this idea. Ross has given us the money to have a better life, and I know that Matty is keen to move. Lauren is more cautious, like me. The young can be so avaricious. Matty wants the full Monty; the swimming pool, the tennis court and the games room. Me, I'm just happy to stay where I am and hire a Marie and a Marcel instead. I cannot stand the thought of having to move all our possessions out of the house where we have lived for so long and brought up our children. James wants to leave all the furniture behind for the next tenant and buy more. I'm sure I will feel like a fish out of water rattling around an enormous unfamiliar mansion, complete with brand new gadgets that I do not know how to use. Matty seems keen to start sixth form at a public school. I'm worried that he will not fit in, but realise the old boy network it provides in later life will be invaluable when it comes to choosing a career. Lauren wants to give up her job and backpack around the world with friends. I am horrified at the thought, but realise that she is young and confident. I must not hold her back.

Sally, the estate agent attached to Burtenshaw's of Richmond is virtually falling over herself with smiles and sycophancy as she shows us around one property after another, mentally rubbing her hands together at the prospect of two per cent commission. All I can see are large, echoing rooms which Ross will never grace with his presence. I am all for giving up and going back to Suffolk as we follow her to the last property on the day's list, Coopers, a six bedroomed family home which comes into view through the front windscreen as we turn down a private tree-lined road. There are only two other properties along the road, which is fringed with fields to the side and lush woodland to the rear.

"This looks ideal." James follows Sally's Audi down the driveway to the porticoed front door. "What do you think?"

"I like the location." I look around me. "It's not too big

either. I didn't like all those massive mansions standing in acres of grounds; it's not *me*.

"It's got a pool at the back apparently, so the kids will be pleased."

James switches off the engine and we follow Sally inside. My heels echo on the black and white floor tiles in the spacious hallway.

"This property is empty. It is owned by a Mr and Mrs Cooper who emigrated to Australia. It's a steal at nine hundred and ninety five thousand."

Sally sounds desperate now, but I like what I see. There are three reception rooms, a large kitchen with virtually new units, a family room, a study, and a downstairs cloakroom. Upstairs I find six bedrooms, three with en-suite shower rooms, and two further bathrooms. Everywhere is decorated in pleasing pastel shades. I cannot see a thing wrong anywhere.

"Wait until you see the gardens." Sally picks up on my approving glances. "There's a swimming pool too."

"Will they take an offer?" James looks at me and I grin.

"I expect they will." Sally nods encouragingly.

Lauren decides she wants a temporary base while she makes travel plans. We give her the keys to our old home on the day we move to Richmond. James says he's outgrown Suffolk, and has secretly always wanted to try for a headmastership in one of the London schools. He's living his dream, and I'm glad. We will keep up with the rental payments until Lauren leaves for her world trip. The house has so many memories for us, and it is a real wrench when I close the front door for the last time. Our daughter reminds us to keep a bedroom for her at Coopers, and I let her know that she will be welcome anytime and can decorate her new room exactly how she wants to. Lauren is growing up; we must let her go her own way.

After a few months settling in, Matty takes to public school like the proverbial duck to water. He brings home new friends for tea named Rupert and Sebastian. The boys are exquisitely polite and gracious. Little by little his old life begins to erode, but I keep him mindful of his uncle Ross; the one who paid for it all in the first place.

When the summer arrives Izzy phones to say she is feeling well, and would like to visit. I look forward to seeing my sister again with an eagerness I have not felt for years. I ask her for a photo of Ross as a keepsake, and she replies that yes, of course, she will bring me one. As I replace the receiver I think of just the right place to hang his picture; up on the wall near the bowl of fruit on the dining room table. If truth be told I have never been able to eat a Golden Delicious apple since 1970 without thinking of him.

CHAPTER 46

CLARE

SHE LOOKS THE epitome of health as she parks her hired Audi in the driveway and steps out of the car. She is tanned and elegant, and has a more rounded figure. Izzy smiles from ear to ear as we embrace.

"Clare! You've no idea how much I've been looking forward to meeting up with you!"

Her perfume is light and expensive. I can hardly believe it is the same person who lay so still and devoid of spirit in her hospital bed.

"Come in and make yourself at home!" I kiss her and suddenly feel like crying for all the lost years. "It's great to see you looking so well!"

"I still go for my check-ups, but everything seems to be working as it should." Izzy chuckles and brings out a bag from the back of the car and gives it to me. "There's some presents for everyone in here, and that photo of Ross you wanted." She puts an arm around my shoulders. "Come on,

I like it that she admires my house. She follows me as I take a tray of tea and biscuits out through the patio doors down to the pool area.

"Did you bring your swimming costume?"

I plonk the tray down and wave to James as he swims up and down.

Izzy shakes her head.

"I never was too keen on swimming; I'm happy to watch."

"It's a wonder James and Matty haven't grown gills." I chuckle. "Lauren's still trotting around the world, but you'll see Matty soon. He'll be home from his Saturday job in a couple of hours. He works at the local leisure centre at weekends."

Izzy settles down in one of the loungers, pours herself some tea, and gives me a parcel.

"This is for you, to go with the photo."

I carefully tear the tissue paper and give a gasp of surprise to see a platinum record of Kick's last album in a frame. Izzy smiles at me.

"As soon as Ross died, sales of the album went sky high. I want you to have it."

"No, it's too much." I shake my head.

"Ross would have been pleased for you to take it." Izzy hands over his photo in a matching frame. "And it's what I want."

"I shall treasure both of them always." I hold the frames to my chest. "What wonderful presents!"

"You missed out on so much; it's payback time." Izzy laughs.

"Only through my own stupidity." I sigh as I stir my tea.

"Not just about you and me. You loved him; I know that." Izzy looks at me directly. "I'm your sister; you don't have to bullshit me."

"Yes I did love him." I nod. "But it occurred to me that all this time I've been in love with the guy I met at the Isle of Wight festival in nineteen seventy. Happily I realised just in time that I've got the real thing here at home."

I hope the lie sounds convincing. I look over at James who is tactfully still swimming and leaving us to chat, and realise that neither Izzy nor James will ever know the real depth of my feeling for Ross. However, thankfully the explanation seems to mollify my sister, who watches as James climbs out of the pool and then executes a perfect dive.

"You've got a good man there, Clare."

"I know. He's finally been given a headmastership; he'll be starting at The Edenleigh Boys' Academy in September. I'm very proud of him."

I smile at James, as he hauls himself out of the water. "Hi Izzy; great to see you!" He towels himself dry, gives Izzy a peck on the cheek, and sits down with us. "How are you feeling now?"

"Better than I've done for ages." Izzy takes a sip of tea. "I've brought a little something for you."

"For me?" James looks surprised.

"Yes. What do you think of this?"

I can see my husband's look of interest as Izzy takes out a flat parcel from her bag, again wrapped in tissue paper, and hands it to him. As he tears the wrapping I can see a sheet of paper under glass with what looks to be a poem written on it. After James has read it he looks up at Izzy.

"It's beautiful."

"Ross wrote it a few weeks before he died." Izzy sighed. "He was going to set it to music and record it with the band, but alas it will now always stay as a poem. He wrote it with you in mind, so you must have it."

"I don't know what to say."

James looks at the poem again before handing it to me. As I read it I can feel tears wanting to spring to the back of my eyes, but manage to push them away.

Your love is an apple,
In the heat of the day,
Its juice runs too sweet,
For me ever to stay.

Like a bud in the spring,
Before the bloom of the flower,
I pick you too soon,
And the apple tastes sour.

Not one bite
Can I take from the fruit,
I yearn for another,
And love you as a brother.

Don't want to fight
Don't want to cause any pain
But love is my ripened peach
Soft flesh on the tree within reach.

So now you know,
What I tried to do,

I set her free,
And she looked straight at you.

Out of the corner of my eye I can see James watching me as I read. I stand up, kiss the top of his head, and gather up Izzy's gifts to take inside for safekeeping. As I climb the steps back up to the patio I wonder how many people there are in this world who actually *do* marry their first love, for they are the lucky ones indeed.

THE END

If you have enjoyed this story, you may like 'A Marriage of Convenience' also by Stevie Turner.

D.G Kaye's review of 'A Marriage of Convenience':

"Turner has a gift for creating engrossing family drama stories and fleshing out strong characters who draw us into their stories and emotions.

In this tale we are introduced to Sophie, a university student, who is offered an unusual opportunity to marry Gerrie, an aspiring musician who is a fellow student at her school; he's looking for someone who will marry him to give him legal status to stay in the U.K. legally to pursue his musical career. A large sum of money comes with the offer which makes it quite a tempting one.

What transpires from their marriage of convenience turns out to be a lasting love, along with an emotional rollercoaster for both Sophie and Gerrie from the beginning when they both, first have to inform their parents about the sudden marriage, and continues with the drama that ensues throughout their marriage (no spoilers). Suffice it to say, that the plot thickens when Gerrie hatches a plot to extract money from his wealthy parents to start up a band and take it on the road, which backfires because Gerrie's parents had bigger dreams of him taking over the family business, so there was no other way his parents would freely hand him over the money for a pipedream. This leaves Gerrie with no option but to go through with his alternate plan which ultimately winds up jeopardizing his family.

The story continues to build with many tribulations as the couple's plight to gain funds gets sticky, and Gerrie and Sophie are faced with dramatic family woes. As the years pass and their family grows, grief that is hidden but never forgotten plays a big part in their quest to regain their family unit and in doing so, find forgiveness for the baddies who had turned their lives upside down."

Other Books by Stevie Turner:

The Pilates Class
A House Without Windows
For the Sake of a Child
Lily: A Short Story
No Sex Please, I'm Menopausal!
A Rather Unusual Romance
The Daughter-in-Law Syndrome
Revenge
The Noise Effect
Repent at Leisure
Life: 18 Short Stories
Waiting in the Wings
Mind Games
A Marriage of Convenience